"So renowned Corberrins! You are very welcome here, my friends, and I hope our food is to your liking. Corisande, I believe: you are more beautiful than your posters, my dear, and it is hard to believe that one so attractive and young could be so talented! And you are Berneson."

Berneson nodded, squaring his shoulders and giving the Azuli general a ceremonious nod of the head rather than a bow. The alien did not offer to shake hands or grip forearms, fortunately. Berneson was uncomfortable enough, just being here within the lair of the enemy. One slip—one intuitive Azuli guess —and not only their careers but their freedom and very possibly their lives were forfeit.

andrew j. offutt is a native of Kentucky, where he still makes his home with his wife and four children. Winning a college science fiction contest started him on his career as an author. *Evil Is Live Spelled Backwards* and *The Castle Keeps* are among his other books.

THE LAUREL-LEAF LIBRARY brings together under a single imprint outstanding works of fiction and non-fiction particularly suitable for young adult readers, both in and out of the classroom. The series is under the editorship of M. Jerry Weiss, Distinguished Professor of Communications, Jersey City State College; Charles F. Reasoner, Professor of Elementary Education, New York University; and Carolyn W. Carmichael, Associate Professor, Department of Communication Sciences, Kean College of New Jersey.

The Galactic Rejects

andrew j. offutt

This one's for
Missy, Scotty, Jeff, Chris
—and you, too

Published by
Dell Publishing Co., Inc.
1 Dag Hammarskjold Plaza
New York, New York 10017

Laurel-Leaf Library ® TM 766734, Dell Publishing
Co., Inc.
Reprinted by arrangement with Lothrop, Lee and Shepard
Printed in the United States of America
First Laurel printing—November 1974

Part 1

The Earthsiders

1

"PLEASE REMAIN CALM! REMAIN CALM!"

The voice blared all over the ship, echoing tinnily. Surprisingly, most of the passengers heeded. Most of them at least *acted* calm. They were all en route home from the Azuli front, and had been under fire before. While it was true that none had been aboard a stricken spaceship before, most were aware of the pernicious effect of panic.

Now their transport spacer had been holed, twice, by an Azuli spaceshark. Their transport spacer was dying.

But all were in spacesuits, and helmeted, uniformly and dimly blue-faced behind the tinted plastoc. They had hurried into the cumbersome suits as soon as the Azuli destroyer had been sighted. Then they had waited, all of them, while *Brunner's* captain flashed out his message to the Azuli, again and again.

The spaceshark had ignored the messages, ignored the fact that *Brunner* was a non-combat craft and headed away from the war zone, not toward it.

Brunner was dying. Or already dead.

"THERE ARE SPACEBOATS FOR EVERYONE," the voice blared on, from every speaker. "WOMEN FIRST, PLEASE. THERE IS NO RUSH; REPEAT, NO NEED TO RUSH. AT PRESENT WE ARE TOO

NEAR A PLANETARY MASS TO LAUNCH
BOATS. WE WILL ALL ENTER THEM NOW,
AND WE WILL WAIT—ONLY A FEW MO-
MENTS. PLEASE REMAIN CALM."

"What kind of lovely targets are we going to make
for that shark and its gunners in these—muffin tins?"
the blond girl asked.

Ensign Bularen gave her a small smile. She was
pretty, slim, and nearly as small as his smile, with
very large blue eyes within her helmet. A teen-aged
girl. With a petulant mouth. It was the kind of mouth
that made you wonder whether she was as pretty inside as out. Her voice was petulant, too.

"The Azuli haven't attacked spacepods yet," Bularen told her. "We'll be all right. Just pop in now;
thank you."

She climbed into the hemispherical lifeboat, a four-
person craft with a bench running three quarters
of the way around its padded inner cell. The remaining space was taken up by dials and gauges and simple
controls. She sat facing the ensign, her spacesuit too
big for her. It was bright yellow.

The ensign turned from her as a man hurried up
out of the crowd, another rumpled white spacesuit.
Ensign Bularen frowned, raised a gauntleted hand,
and shook his head.

"I'm sorry sir. You'll have to—"

He broke off as the man before him vanished—

—and appeared in the pod beside the girl. She
jumped a little, startled, and shrank from him.

"Sir," the ensign said, spinning to face him, "you'll
have to—"

But again Bularen broke off as his attention was
diverted. Another man, a bigger and older one, was
trying to push past him into the same spaceboat. The
ensign gripped his suited arm.

"Sir, there are plenty of boats. But you heard the order: it's tradition, that's all. Women first, all right? There is plenty of time and there are plenty of pods."

"That's my daughter in there," the man pleaded, waving a hand at the seated girl in the pod. He looked to be in his late forties. Brown hair, retreating from his forehead as though afraid of his staring eyes. Gray at the temples. And his eyes . . . Bularen shuddered. The man's deep brown eyes looked . . . dead. Burned out.

"Oh," the ensign said. "Well, I guess that makes a dif—"

"No he isn't!" It was the blue-eyed girl. "That nasty man isn't my father! He's just afraid to wait, that's all! Coward!" Her voice rose shrilly.

The man looked beseechingly at her, one hand outstretched. She stared back at him, and there was ice in her wide, sky-colored eyes. The ensign looked grim. His hand tightened on the man's arm.

"Now look sir, you're just going to have to wait. Just stand by for a moment. I *must* go in this pod, you see, but if no women come to board it, we'll get in together. All right?"

"No!"

The middle-aged man moved with surprising swiftness, swinging a hard blow that slammed into the ensign's midsection. As the young officer started to double over, the man half-turned him and shoved him violently backward. A woman, hurrying toward the pod out of the crowd of passengers on the airless ship, fell over him. Her helmet banged the deck, but of course the thermoplastoc did not break. With the magnetic grapples on their heavy shoes separated from the deck, she and the ensign floated. She flailed wildly.

The man swung and vaulted into the pod with

youthful agility. His gloved hand slapped a lever down and leaped out to jerk open a small, curved cover. Beneath it was a button, red. He pushed it.

The spacepod's lid banged shut and the automatic toggles spun. At the same time, the tiny craft shivered and rolled, trembling. Then it shot out of its port, away from *Brunner* and into the intense darkness of space.

The man leaned back. The front of his white spacesuit rose and fell rapidly with his breathing, creasing and rumpling and recreasing again and again.

"We can't leave the ship without a crewman!" This from the man who had disappeared/reappeared in the pod, and he was yelling. "We'll—"

"We just did," he was told quietly.

"You cowardly old MAN!" the girl shouted. "You COWARD!"

He was doing things with the controls. Air hissed. A small panel came alight, bluely. A needle swung, trembled, stopped. The man nodded and opened his faceplate, took a breath, and nodded again. He began undogging his helmet from his suit.

Not until then did he raise his flat brown eyes to the girl. She stared at them, frowning, and her mouth closed.

"My wife died on Siniras, and I got this." He bowed his head as he removed the space helmet, showing her a hairless place in his scalp, with a raised line of skin there, like a welt. "The Azuli. I think I've given enough to this war. A nasty little girl is entitled to a seat on a lifeboat, and a war veteran with a wound and a wife killed by the Azuli isn't, is that it? You just shut up." His voice was as disconcerting as his eyes, all throaty and very quiet and so terribly calm-sounding. As dead as his eyes.

"I'm a veteran too, you nasty old man!" Her voice was high and loud, going shrill as she drew off her own helmet. Her hair tumbled out. It was yellowish blond, what the poetically inclined would have called golden, and there was a lot of it. Her eyes scorned him, flashed at him, their blue becoming electric. "*I* was on that Azuli planet, too. *I* was on Siniras! I—"

"Suff, I know," he said. His voice was not all that deep, but he was a man, and older; his control of it made it sound deeper. "I know. You're Corisande, you're sixteen, you're a poltie, and you're about as dependable as the wind on Talmur. And they sent you back, put you on that ship back to Earth, because you're a moody, melodramatic *brat* and they couldn't depend on you. Besides—your powers are failing."

"They are NOT!"

Her helmet sprang from her lap to rush at him. He slapped it away—and bent forward to slap her, with his other hand. It was not a hard blow, but more like that a doting father bestows on his daughter, rather reluctantly.

Corisande, aged sixteen, moody, melodramatic, poltie brat, commenced to cry.

The two men looked at each other.

"You're not going to call me a coward too, are you, Berneson? After you teleported into the pod?" The middle-aged man grinned. His eyes refused to cooperate, remaining flat and dead.

Without his helmet, the man he called Berneson looked maybe thirty, maybe twenty-nine. Faded gray eyes, swift-moving and seldom still. A thin face with pronounced cheekbones. Curly hair, dark but not quite black. The eyes, strangely, were full of humor and already there were the crow's-feet of frequent laughter at their edges. He shook his head.

"Berneson," the older man went on reflectively. "You're twenty-five years old—you look older; too bad—and a teeporter. And you're opposed to the Earth-Azul war. They had to drag you up here by proclaiming you a Government Resource. So . . . you footled your way out."

Berneson shrugged, trying to twist on the bench to stretch his long thin legs. "Shuff," he acknowledged. "You're a reese, huh?"

A nod: "I'm a receiver."

"Right." Berneson nodded. "I'm with you, flainer. A coward. I didn't want to come, and I was sent anyhow. They put the G-R tag on me, just as you said. I've been there: both Egla and Siniras. And I'm still alive." He shrugged a shoulder that looked bony beneath his bulky spacesuit. "I saw no reason to wait for a seat on this pod, either." He looked very comfortable, relaxed.

"You're a Martian," the girl said, peeping up between her fingers.

Berneson chuckled. "Born on Earth. Been on Mars since I was ten. How'd you know—are you a reeser as well as a poltie?"

She shook her head. "Your accent. You say 'shuff' instead of 'suff,' and you called him 'flainer.' That's a Martian slangword. Almost all your s's sound like sh, too."

"Our little detective," Berneson said, with neither warmth nor rancor.

"You were wise to get into this pod," the other man told him. He was frowning at the instruments. "They were lying to us. There were *not* enough pods on *Brunner*. All of us wouldn't have got to go. The captain was checking a list even while he was telling us to be calm. He was underlining names on the passenger manifest: people to leave behind." He gazed steadily at Berneson. "He'd already passed your name, Berneson."

"And?" Berneson's tone seemed unconcerned, but his eyes twitched.

"You'd have been left."

Berneson sighed. "Umm. I'm not a valuable Government Resource anymore," he said, twisting on the bench. He tucked his left foot behind the right.

"Not a valuable one, no. Because you were no longer valuable to the war effort."

The girl looked up, sniffling. "And you?"

"I don't know," the older man said. "He hadn't got down to my name yet. I decided not to wait. I had an idea he'd underline it." He shook his gray-templed head. "We're a real trio! A fading poltie—a sixteen-year-old brat they sent back because she couldn't be depended on, even *before* her Power started fading."

"It isn't!" Her space helmet quivered, started to rise. He leaned toward her.

"You try telekinning that thing at me again and I'll slap you again, girl. Harder."

"You'd *slap* me? A girl?"

"Yes, I would, Corisande. You can't hide behind being a girl; you can't have it both ways. Somebody should have slapped you long ago."

Helmet and girl subsided, relaxing or appearing to. She glowered at him. "It isn't fading," she said. Quietly.

"All poltergeisters are temperamental." Berneson said, "like race horses. Very emotional. That's part of what makes them polties."

She looked at him, obviously not certain whether to be grateful or angry.

The other man was ignoring her, looking at Berneson. "And a teleport who wanted to teeport to all the wrong places."

Berneson shrugged, grinning at him.

"Teleported into the nurses' barracks, didn't you, Berneson. Fun and games. And that was just the *last* of your tricks!"

"Get out of my mind!"

"I'm not in your cynical little mind, Berneson. You're broadcasting. And it's mostly 'I—I—I.' I don't crawl into minds; I just receive thoughts, what you might call 'loud' thoughts. Anyhow: so they busted you, and sent you back—to Detent. And you teeported in here. Lucky for you I came along; that ensign was mad and would have dragged you out." He was sneering.

Berneson shrugged. He was leaning back, looking quite comfortable, half smiling. "I'd just have popped into another pod," he said. "But you—" he grinned and his voice became scathing. "*You* tried to be Miss Poltergeist's daddy." He gestured at the girl. "To get a seat on the same pod. Makes you better, I suppose."

"Is—is your name Rinegar?" the girl asked, and both men looked at her. "Is it?"

"Look at his face," Berneson said. "Sure it is. What do you know about him, little girl?"

"I'm not a little girl!" But she continued gazing at the older man: Rinegar. Her expression was sympathetic, now. "He is a reeser, of course, a telepathic receiver. And his wife was a sender. They were spies: the perfect telepath team. Everybody's heard of *them*, just like the Rameys and their daughter. She psi-sent, and he received." She nodded at Rinegar. "And . . . he got wounded. And she was . . . caught."

"By the *Azuli?*" Berneson's brows were down.

Rinegar turned his staring eyes away, to the controls and dials and gauges. "Shut up. Shut up. Shut up."

Frowning, Berneson asked, "What happened?"

The girl's mouth opened to reply, but it was Rinegar who spoke. The words came out of him like sawdust in freefall. Slow. Dry. Harsh.

"They tortured her. I heard—I *felt*—every second of it. I FELT them torturing her," he said, his voice rising, the control faltering, "and I felt everything in her mind. And I COULDN'T MOVE!"

Berneson shuddered. He looked at the girl. "They . . . killed her?"

She nodded.

"Tortured her to death," Rinegar said. "And I reesed every minute of it. Every *second!*" He banged a veined hand onto the padded bulkhead; there was hardly any sound at all. But the sensitive little lifeboat lurched into a new course.

"He wasn't any good to them after that," the girl said very quietly. "Haven't you heard of him?"

Berneson shook his head. His cocky smile was gone as he gazed at the other man.

"The head wound," Rinegar muttered, not looking at them. "The wound. It messed up my Power. So they sent me back. Pensioned out, with a little speech. Rinegar: thanks for all the years. Thanks for all the danger you've been through and all the information you got us. Sorry about your wife. Here's a nice medal to replace her. Go home, Rinegar. We don't need you anymore . . . we don't want you anymore." His voice was flat, dull.

"You reesed both of us," Berneson pointed out.

The girl swung her head to him with an angry look. "Why'd you have to—"

"A fluke," Rinegar said, almost snarling. "It just happened. But it doesn't always, not anymore."

Berneson made an ugly noise. "Sparm!" he growled, and the girl affected to look shocked. "Did you fake it, Rinegar, or did you go over the edge?"

Rinegar jerked his head to stare at the other man, then lurched across the tiny space separating them. The little lifepod spun. Rinegar's hand closed on Berneson's throat—

—and he was yanked back, hurled back against the padded, curving side of the craft. And held there, as if his body were charged and magnetically imprisoned against the surface behind him. His eyes rolled to the girl. She was staring intently at him, looking very tense and stiff. She hadn't moved.

"Let me go!"

"Promise," she said, in a voice strained with her psi-effort. "Promise, Rinegar: leave him alone! Listen! Listen Berneson, you too, listen. He's right. We're rejects, all three of us. Sent back because we aren't good enough. You talked about my being emotional—suff, that's right, that's it with us polties. But what about the two of you? You, Berneson, grinning and sneering, using your powers for silly pranks in the middle of a war, and still grinning and sneering. What are you covering up, Berneson?" And before he could answer, frowning, she swung her head to Rinegar.

"And you! Acting as if there's something wrong with emotion! Your Power isn't gone, any more than mine is. You underwent something horrible, and you loved your wife. You—you took a direct hit in the emotions, that's what. Why should we try to cover it up? We three can't pretend with each other. We're . . . emotional cripples." She bit her lip. "We're not good enough. As badly as they need psi's in the war with Azul, they sent us three back. Now . . . now we're stuck with each other. We're—"

And she was crying again, her shoulders bowed and jerking, her head down, hair streaming. Abruptly Rinegar sagged and slid down the bulkhead. Her mental hold on his body was broken; she was no longer concentrating.

He and Berneson gazed at her. Then Rinegar looked at the younger man, and Berneson dropped his eyes.

"I'm . . . sorry, Rinegar. That was vicious."

"Also true," Rinegar told him. "Did I hurt you?"

"No."

The girl looked up. She was fighting her tears, fighting them hard. The men watched the droplets spring from her eyes, lift from her cheeks, collect in mid-air. It was her Power, they knew; the pod was equipped with simulagrav, about nine-tenths Earth standard. The collected tears dropped to the deck where six spacebooted feet were planted close together.

"Where are we?" she asked.

Rinegar shrugged. "Who knows. No one told us."

"You don't know how to read those things?" the other man asked, nodding at the control console.

Rinegar shook his head. "I know how to read this," he said, tapping a greenish gauge, "and this," tapping a winking amber light, "and this." Another gauge with a double needle. "That light says we're caught in the gravity of a planet. As the captain said."

"The captain," Berneson muttered, gazing at nothing. "He underlined his own name, of course."

"What planet?" Corisande's voice shot up the scale, bouncing off C over high C: the sound of hysteria.

Again Rinegar shook his head. "Don't know."

"The dials?" Berneson was hunched forward, peer-

ing at them with eyes that said plainly they were telling him nothing.

"We're falling fast toward the planet. The other
gauge says that in a few seconds the boat will take
over. When the amber light goes red."

"We won't . . . crash?"

"No. The pod will land itself. We'll have to be very
still."

"Then what?" Now her voice was woefully tiny. A
sixteen-year-old's voice. Scared.

Rinegar shrugged. "Then we're there."

"Where?"

"Wherever we are. On a planet. Look, I don't
know."

"Suppose it's an Azuli planet!" Berneson's hands
were leaving sweatmarks on the baggy trousers bond-
ed to his boots. "We'd have been better off if you
hadn't—"

"Good chance," Rinegar interrupted. "Or there's
also a good chance that it's an unpeopled world. Or
uninhabitable. Airless."

"Please . . ." Corisande was whimpering.

"We'll know in about thirty minutes," Rinegar told
her.

And they jerked and fell together as the boat took
over its own con. There were no retros, not on a
deepspace lifeboat. The brick-sized computer merely
ordered the hand-sized antigrav unit, its coils spider-
webbing the entire area between the pod's two hulls,
to start resisting the gravity of the planet that had
captured them.

There were no portholes. They could not see. They
felt little motion, although they knew they were going
"down," now, relative to the unknown planet. They
sat in silence, staring at each other with glassy eyes
and tight faces.

Time slid by, creeping like oil on cold metal.

The boat touched something. The red light went out.

An amber one blinked on.

"Are—are we down?"

Rinegar nodded at her. "We're down. No trouble at all."

"We're down," Berneson muttered. "Somewhere in space, somewhere on an unknown planet." He shook his head. "No, no. No trouble at *all!*"

"Now we wait," Rinegar said, as though Berneson hadn't spoken at all. "Either this red light comes on and says we stay here, or the green says it's safe to leave."

"Leave? How can we *leave?*" the girl cried. "This is just a spacepod, a lifeboat."

"I didn't mean leave the *planet,*" Rinegar said in that same quiet, controlled voice. "We aren't leaving this planet; understand that. The pod can't do that. No, I meant that if the green light comes on, it's safe to leave the pod. Out onto the planet."

"Safe?"

"Safe to breathe. After that . . . it's up to us."

They looked at one another.

The water on the nameless planet was water, oxygen mingled at the molecular level with twice as much hydrogen to form a liquid. The sun was a warm yellow-white. The air was breathable. The scanners said so.

The pod's light came on: green.

They left their spacesuits behind, Rinegar, Corisande, Berneson. They—or rather Rinegar—took the one pistol the pod had boasted. They walked out onto the new world.

"How beautiful," the girl breathed, bringing her hands together in a gesture that was almost a clap. "How *beautiful!*"

The sky was the color of her eyes, strewn with cirrus clouds like floating white islands on a pale blue sea. Their sun-gilded edges were nearly the color of her hair, a delicate, rippling mass that fell down her back to her waist like a white-gold cloak of some thin and loosely woven fabric. Silk, perhaps, or its laboratory-created successor.

The tall trees were mostly thick, rough trunk shaded by green canopies; dark green, like Berneson's leggings below his bottle-green tunic. The distant mountains were purple, a misty purple resembling the color of the girl's loose-sleeved tunic; their tops were mists of blue-gray-white, like Berneson's eyes. The peaks of those far mountains nudged the sky.

There was a great deal of green, in an assortment of shades. It was virginal-looking, as though no one had ever cut the trees or plowed the land. The sky, Rinegar remarked, was clear, as though there was no polluting industry on this planet. They glanced from the sky to one another, their eyes clearly stating their uncertainty. Was a clear, smokeless and smogless sky a good sign or bad?

Rinegar, who wore black boots and charcoal leggings and tunic of a lighter gray, almost slate, looked about. He turned slowly, eventually completing a small circle in his footsteps. A worm and two diminutive insects and countless even tinier creatures perished beneath his turning feet. Was this the advent of man on this planet: death?

"Pastoral," he said. "Lovely."

"People?" Berneson asked, thrusting back the thick dark sickle of hair that preferred his forehead to his crown. "You reese any people, Rinegar?"

Rinegar shook his head. "No. Why don't you reconnoiter? You can teeport around and—"

"In the first place," the younger man interrupted, "I can 'port just as far as you can reese, I imagine."

"About a half-kilometer," Rinegar said.

"Right. In the second place, I don't dare 'port *any*-place here. I can't be sure where I'd land, or on what. In the middle of a lake, or a fire, or right on top of a snake, or a meter or two from some beastie, or—"

"Teleport out of it," Corisande said with a shrug.

He grinned, shaking his head. "Doesn't work that way. Look Sandy—"

"My name is not Sandy."

"Yes well, Corisande is an awful lot of name."

She stared at him a moment, then sighed exaggeratedly. "Well, if you *must* shorten it, call me Cory."

"Cory, then. Look, I'm not going to take the chance. A teeporter 'ports to where he can *see,* or someplace he's been and knows, so that he knows where he's going to land. I could bounce from here to over there under that tree—that one yonder with all the fringe hanging down like a beard—and I might land on a snake, or a rock. Suppose it was the rock, and I fell and broke my leg. I couldn't shift mental gears and teeport away fast enough."

"All right," Rinegar said, "all right. Let's decide. Do we stay here, or walk? We aren't going anywhere in this pod." He jerked his hand at the spaceboat, which looked very small even as close as three or four meters away. "This planet's gravity is stronger than the pod's thrust. I can feel it. I'm a little heavier here. The pod brought us down like a parachute, resisting enough to keep us from cracking up. But parachutes don't go back up."

"I can't see why not," Corisande said, gazing reproachfully at the pod. "If this had been someplace like Jupiter, for instance, or Kraken, we'd have been smashed all over the ground! Seems to me spacepods ought to be able to be converted into—well, airskims or something like that."

"They weren't designed for that purpose," Berneson said. "A spacepod's a highly temporary little coffin to keep you alive in space. *In space.* Until a ship comes along and picks up the pods and their survivors. They weren't designed to go landing on planets."

And suddenly both he and Corisande were staring at Rinegar. He had brought them here. It was he who had hit the Eject button and sent them whisking away from the holed spaceship before they should have done. The other pods might well have been picked up by now. The other survivors of *Brunner* might well be on their way to Earth, or to some intermediate planet where they'd be picked up by another transport and taken home. As to the three psi's . . . they would be famous. Infamous. Outlaws. They'd jumped ship in a spacepod designed for four, just the three of them, and one less person had been able to escape *Brunner*.

And as if that were not entirely enough, they were now on a completely unknown—however beautiful— planet, with one gun and no transportation or instruments, not even a compass or a stove to heat food—if there was food.

Corisande and Berneson stared at Rinegar.

"Well," the girl said at last, "we're here, and that's that." She looked up at the friendly sky, around at the rolling grassy plain and its trees. Then she hopped and hopped again, her tunic fluttering, her legs long and slim in wet-shiny black tights and silver-striped black boots.

"Only about one-point-one gee or less, I'd say," she decided after a third hop. "Just a little over one standard gravity."

Rinegar shrugged. "Whatever, it's ours now. We won't be leaving. So—as I started to say, we can just loll around here, waiting to see who or what finds us. Or we can—start walking."

"Where?" she asked, noticing for the first time that he had a regrown left thumb. Something had gone a bit wrong, and it was a paler color than the rest of his hand. "Where? Which direction?"

"Who cares? We can draw straws, or close our eyes and turn and point. Does it matter?"

"Sure," Berneson said. "We could walk from now until the middle of next year. And/or starve."

"I wonder how long a year is?" Corisande murmured. Now that she was out of the pod and had stared at Rinegar and got that out of her system, she seemed unaffected by the helplessness—if not hopelessness—of their situation.

"Berneson," Rinegar began, and paused. "Uh, what are you called?"

"Berneson," the other man said stiffly, then shrugged. "Ah, call me Bernie."

"Bernie, look around. Trees. Grass. Breathable air—a little heady, isn't it? More oxygen than we're used to, just a bit. No pollutants, I'll bet. Nice gravity—and look, that's an earthworm. This is a people-type planet. We won't starve here. There'll be animals, and fruits and things."

Cory's eyes left the sky and her chin came down. "People?" Her voice sounded more fearful than hopeful.

"Maybe."

"Let's go—that way." She pointed. Her suggested goal was a thin line of trees, kilometers away. Uncertain of the trees' height, they could not be sure of the distance.

Rinegar looked at Berneson. "Matter to you, Bernie?"

"No."

"All right, Cory. We go your way."

"Am I the leader?"

Rinegar laughed.

He did not, she noticed, have a very pretty laugh, and his eyes hardly participated. The laugh was raspy and throaty, flat like his voice and his eyes. If there were such creatures as zombies, they would surely look and talk like Rinegar.

"We haven't a leader," he said. "We're a team. But I am the oldest."

She shrugged. "I'm the youngest, too. So what? And I suggested a direction. Oh, and I guess I'm in charge of defense, too. I have the Power."

"Listen, little girl, what defense? Defense against what?" Rinegar sighed, shaking his head. "I'll know the moment we're within a half-kilometer of any brain large enough to need defending against. And I've got this."

He slapped the pistol. It fired coveys of needles, swarms of them that did nasty things to whatever they hit, provided the target was composed of living cells. It had been the only weapon on the lifepod because the ensign was to have come aboard.

"And I won't need defending either, thanks," the younger man said. "I can teeport out of the way as fast as you can duck—and farther, too." He vanished—

—reappeared beside the pod, smiled, vanished—

—and was back in his previous position before the grass could straighten in his tracks.

Her full lower lip became fuller.

"Then would you two big strong men protect *me?* And come on, let's go and see what dark menace lurks behind yon line of trees. Maybe there's a yellow brick road."

Very conscious that they were walking into the totally unknown, they began walking.

3

The road wasn't yellow brick. But it was a road.

Mostly it was dirt, and pocks, and potholes. And it meandered, as if it had been laid out by a nervous serpent. With hiccups.

But it *was* a road, and that *was* a wheelmark, however thin and treadless, and that meant—people?

No, not necessarily. Not necessarily people. Intelligent creatures, then, who had invented the wheel and were more settled than nomadic, hence the road.

Without saying anything, they looked at one another, and at the road, and they followed it.

The grass bordering the road looked like grass, and weeds. Earth grass; Kentucky or Illinois or Ohio grass, not the strange scrubby stuff that pushes up out of the white dustlike sand of places such as Florida, or the weird twisting and spiky stuff that finally emerged from China's trinitite plains. The earth—no no, not *earth;* the soil, then. The soil appeared very dark, rich.

Among three sturdy weed stalks they saw a complicated, classical-looking spiderweb occupied by an eye-ball-sized, fat yellow arachnid with a patterned scaling of greenish markings quite similar to that of the weed stalks. Its problems, apparently, were few. It merely laid out its web and sat around until this or that insect blundered into it. It had to work for its food, but it didn't have to hunt for it.

There were earthworms, juicy ones, and nearly transparent green bounce-fliers like grasshoppers, and bugs that made noises like hoarse crickets. (Cory's description. Crickets, Berneson pointed out, made their noises with their legs. Nailfile-legged crickets, then, she said carelessly, and Rinegar almost smiled.)

And there were birds, mostly brown and gray with some black and drab, although once Cory saw one that was as green as the broad field of legumey stuff on their right. She shouted and pointed just as it swooped in for a landing twenty meters away. The men didn't see it; its coloration aided it to vanish the instant it was in the grass. But from the trees another bird answered Cory's cry: *peeWEE peeWEE,* he called, and *peeWEE* again.

"Pee wee to you too," Cory said, smiling.

They saw the barn first, and then the house, and several other buildings. All were built of wood.

The house was mostly white, or had been the last time its clapboards were painted. The barn, too, was white, and it had been painted—or whitewashed—more recently. The outbuildings were unpainted wood, except for the shiny one that must have been tin. Then they saw the animals: milk cows, mostly red and white. Like Ayrshires—except for the manes. And a horse. Or perhaps it was a zebra, or a little of both. He had a stiffly erect forelock, red, and no mane to speak of, and his whisk-broom tail was red-tufted. He was gray.

"A horse," Cory said, "in sports clothes!"

Next they saw the man.

Not a creature. He was a man.

He wore a broad sunhat and a sleeveless gray coverall and he was sitting on something with lots of very shiny and very thin wheels. No; they were pointed-edged discs, twenty or thirty of them in a double row just behind and beneath his raised seat, under his feet and flanking them.

The discs turned as he rode along—sitting on a metal seat between two big spoked wheels of iron—and they were biting into the soil. The man was very dark, reddish-brown. His machine was pulled by another gray horse with red crest and tail tip.

"What's he doing?" Cory asked.

"Discing," Ringer told her. They had stopped, and Ringer appeared very alert, as though listening. Which he was, of course—with his mind. "Seriously, that machine is a disc harrow. He calls it a disc. It pulverizes the soil."

"It's already been plowed," Berneson observed.

"Why?" Cory asked, watching the farmer with her head cocked a little to one side.

"To prepare the ground for planting," Ringer explained. "You don't just throw seed into plowed furrows, you know. It's later summer here. He's turned under, with the plow, what's left of the crop he had there. Beans, or like beans. He'll sow some cereal crop on it now, like wheat or rye, for the winter. A cover crop, to cover the soil. In the spring he'll turn *that* under, and plant his beans, his money crop."

"He's thinking all that?" Cory was staring at the farmer's back. It was broad, and dark in the middle, as though there were a strip up the center of his coverall: sweat.

"No. Some of it I knew. He—he's barely reesable.

A very contented, complacent man. Anyhow—you don't know much, do you. *Stop that!"*

She stared at him. "You knew?"

Ringegar nodded. "You were about to throw a clod at me. Make one jump up and fly at me, I mean, with your mind. You were emoting; of course I knew it."

"Why don't you keep your nasty reesing out of my mind!"

He chuckled. "I wasn't *in* your mind, Corisande. I have very conscientiously stayed out of your mind. Yours too, Bernie. But you'll have to learn control, Cory. You lose your temper, get excited, and then your brain broadcasts. Try some control; it'll be good for you. Everyone should stop being a child sooner or later. Nearly everyone broadcasts, you see, when there's emotion envolved. Anger, fear."

"Think sweet thoughts," Berneson muttered, not grinning for a change, "and *then* throw clods, little girl."

"I'm *not*—you're saying that on purpose!"

"I don't say anything by accident," Berneson said. "I control my tongue. Do you?"

"We are on a strange planet," Ringegar said, throwing the words into the tenseness between them, "and we've found people. And you two—lord, Berneson, and *you* call *her* a little girl!"

Trembling a little, her plump lower lip suddenly held very tight, Corisande stared at Berneson, glanced at Ringegar. She heaved an angry sigh. Then she started walking, like a wind-up soldier. Marching along in high-kneed stomps beside the plowed field. Worms wiggled at her from the upturned dirt that had suddenly ceased being a haven for them and their all-important aeration of the soil.

"I'll go see if Mister Farmer is any nicer to talk

with than you two nasties," she shot back. Stomp stomp.

Berneson, frowning, started forward with his mouth open to call to her.

The older man stopped him with a hand on his arm. "Let her go. We'll see how Miss Snotnose bridges the communication gap."

"The—" Then Berneson grinned. "Of course! He won't be able to understand her! She won't understand him!"

"Right."

Smiling, the two men followed Cory. Her back was very straight, her tunic hem flapping as she stomped away.

Berneson laughed when she turned off the road into the field the farmer was working: the newly turned soil threw her. She fell. He laughed, she twisted to blast him with a look of sheer malice, and a clod of dirt jumped up and rushed at him. He ducked and vanished and was just in front of her, stumbling in the ridged, furrowed, cloddy soil. She squeaked when she turned and saw him so close.

"I just passed up the opportunity to kick your smarty backside," he told her. "Try to learn the same control, will you?"

"You laughed at me!"

"I'll also help you up. But you aren't hurt, and from where I stood it was funny. Try to pretend to be human, why don't you. The sight of other people sprawling is funny—that's why there's so much of it on the holovid entertainments. If they're hurt, *then* you don't laugh. Cory, Cory. You're a pretty girl, and bright, and you've got a Power lots of people would give an arm to have." He chuckled, looking down at her. "Come to think, you telekinesis types don't *need* arms. Anyhow, stop taking everything as a personal affront, Corisande."

"Don't you give me advice!"

She was still half crouching; she'd frozen when he materialized before her. Her backside was toward Rinegar, who was picking his way toward them across the difficult terrain.

"And don't try to get on the good side of me by saying I'm pretty. I know better."

Berneson looked surprised, perhaps a little hurt. Then he shrugged. He put up a hand to push his hair up off his forehead.

"All right, Cory. I tried, remember. But I really couldn't care less whether I'm on your good side or not, if you have one. I can dodge your mind-missiles and teeport myself right up beside you and pop you one and be gone before you can shift mind gears. And you are pretty. Stop playing; a pretty girl who says she isn't is just fishing. You know the truth. Want a hand up?"

She stared up at him. Then: "No!" and she stood. She brushed herself off, wiggling, and looked at him from beneath long lashes. He gazed past her, and she turned as Rinegar reached them.

"Tough walking, isn't it? Worse than half-gee, or double. Better walk, Cory, and stop flouncing."

She glared at him, then at Berneson. "You—you two are *picking* on me! Both of you. Because I'm smaller, and younger, and a girl!"

"Tsk." Rinegar turned those flat, rather frightening eyes on her. "Cory . . . your daddy ever spank you?"

"Don't you dare think of that."

"I wouldn't." Rinegar heaved a deep sigh. "Stop picking on her, Bernie. She's a sweet, misunderstood little princess. What'd you say to her, anyhow?"

"I offered to help her up," Berneson said, "and I told her she's pretty. Next time I'll give her the toe of my boot where her tights're the tightest."

She spun on him. She stood midway between them, on a plowed field, swinging back and forth as each spoke. "I'll—"

"Don't forget what I said," he told her, and vanished—

—and tapped her on the shoulder from behind. She squeaked.

"HOOEYYY!"

All three of them looked up at the new voice. Thirty or forty meters away, the farmer had stopped his single plodding horse and was twisted about on the perforated iron seat of his discer, staring at them. He had a lot of nose.

"HOOEYY! What're you three doing on my land?"

That's what Rinegar "heard;" the other two looked blank at the hail, followed by a stream of gibberish. Rinegar repeated the meaning for them, having got it from the big-nosed farmer's mind. Berneson repeated the farmer's words, as nearly as he could, eliciting a surprised look from the girl.

"Hey—that was good. You sounded just like him."

"My talent," he shrugged, no more able to take compliments than she. "One Power, one talent. And it isn't 'hey' here, it's 'hooey.'" He was twisting the knob on the medallion on his chest. "What'd he say again, Rinegar? Exactly?"

Rinegar told him and Berneson nodded, twisting some more. The farmer shouted again. Corisande thought it time to give him a bright smile, and she waved.

"Hey again," Berneson muttered, concentrating on the medallion, "something . . . something . . . what are you somethings . . . ah, that must be the plural hereabouts . . . doing on my ground. Ground? That must be the word for 'land; property,' I guess." He twisted the smaller central knob on the circular device on his chest.

"The words you didn't get," Rinegar said, "were 'I said,' first, and . . . (I think, Bernie) 'people' the other time. Something like that. He doesn't see us as being too strange, except for our clothing. He isn't at all scared, either."

Click. Berneson nodded. He held the pendant he was fiddling with up before his face.

"Good. It's a pretty simple language. Set to thirty-eight over five. A few more sentences from him and we can converse."

His companions set their translators as he directed, not without respectful looks at the man whose main talent they had thought was japery.

"You'd better answer, Rinegar," Berneson said.

"Call me Jake. All right." Rinegar faced the farmer, threw up a hand, and called out, "We people are on your land." Which the translator almost handled.

"Jake," Cory muttered. *"Jake?"*

The farmer frowned, watching the trio start toward him. He had not, after all, got much of an answer.

"Hi," Cory called. "I'm Corisande."

"Gretting, *something*," the farmer said. *"Something something something something* my land?"

Twisting his medallion, Berneson parroted the words. "Make that .hirty-*nine* over five," he said, and the others made adjustments. They continued walking toward the man, who was sitting unexcitedly on the seat of his farm implement. He and his horse stared. The farmer wore a lot of sideburns, black, and a bushy Zapata sort of mustache, droopy and reddish-brown-black.

"He's wondering if we're with the fair-people," Rinegar said. "Carnival-fair, I mean. "We're dressed funny, he thinks. Funny-off and funny-hoho too, I think. Can't keep his eyes off Cory's tights, but he doesn't seem to be, ah, scandalized." He smiled. "He's wondering how and why and where you got so wet."

"I guess they don't have lab fabrics yet," Berneson said. And grumbled, "I wish he'd say it out loud."

The farmer called again. Unexcitedly, with a modicum of warmth.

"He just did."

"Ah! Thirty-nine-point-two, over four-point-eight," Berneson said, and looked up with a happy grin. He spoke to the man sitting on the discer.

"We people are from the fair-people," he said, or something like that, and the local nodded and smiled as a man does when his guess is confirmed or he recognizes a song or phrase.

Next he asked if they were lost; Berneson admitted that they were lost.

He asked where they'd come from, out of the clear blue sky, and Berneson muttered still another translator adjustment and told him they were out of the clear blue sky.

The translators recorded and relayed to the microcircuitry units in the heads of the three aliens, then made highly "intelligent" and sophisticated surmises, and relayed those, and Berneson tested them and made confirmations and corrections.

It was a ridiculous conversation.

"See Spot run," Cory muttered. But she too concentrated on her translator medallion.

The farmer—Junn Grenn—spoke, and each of them got some of it, with Rinegar translating the thoughts as best he could. The autonomic translators increased vocabulary, relaying to the brains of their

wearers. The words remained in their brains, storing
up like spools of fresh knowledge in the vast mental
library-computer-systems of the three psiers.

"You mean to stand there and tell me you're from
another world? From up there?" The farmer Junn
Grenn waved a hand vaguely, covering most of the
sky.

They nodded, smiling.

"Be drouthed! Really? You're *something* (ing)
me!"

They shook their heads, smiling. No, really. We
aren't kidding you.

"Well, that's something. That's something. We'd really like to talk to somebody from another world. Bet
you could get jobs with the carnival, too. Could you
stay for supper?"

Cory's wide eyes stared. She looked at Rinegar and
Berneson: they were staring, too. Was the man insane? Was it that he didn't believe them at all and was
mocking, or merely stringing along? (If so, he
deserved an acting award. Or a job as psycher.)
Where was his natural xenophobia, his natural antipa-
thy and disbelief?

"Uh . . . I reckon we could stay," Rinegar said.
"He believes us, all right," he muttered to his companions.

Oh yes, Rinegar could see into the man's mind;
Cory had forgot. The fellow must be serious, then.
But—who could conceive of a situation in which the
alien said "Take me to your leader"and the local said
"Suff, suff—but could you stay for supper?"

What did it take to ignition Junn Grenn, anyhow?

"That's real good," Junn Grenn said. "I swear—
I've never met anybody from another world before.
Gally'll be just real pleased, real pleased!" He regarded

the sky, as if searching for their home. "Never! Well. Why don't you just go over to the house there and tell my missus Gally—Galeaneh—to fix up a patch more supper and set some extra places? I've got to get this field finished, but I'll be along."

The trio from another world looked at each other.

"He isn't even . . . I mean, he acts *sort of* excited, as if it's an event," Corisande said. "But—he's not *really* excited."

"He believes us," Rinegar said.

"Is there such a thing," Cory wondered, "as a psychotic haven? Could this be a planet set aside for the hopelessly incurably insane?"

Rinegar: "He's sane."

Berneson: "Maybe . . . maybe these people are used to visitors. But what people? Where are we?"

"We may never know," Rinegar told him. "We were in hyperspace. We came out for a jump, and moments after that the ship was hit. And too near this planet— meaning no one else from the ship will be here. Earth's been so busy with the Azuli ever since we got out of the solar system that we're far from charting and landing on every planet. There hasn't been time for pure research, just spacing around looking for other intelligences. But—no: he's never *heard* of space travel. And we're strange, but he isn't particularly excited about it, and he believes us. He just doesn't raise a Kelvin over anything, evidently. Strange!"

"That the way people talk on another world?"

They nodded, smiling. Junn Grenn smiled back.

4

Seventeen-year-old Junty Grenn (Junn, junior), spent most of the meal with his eyes on Cory.

Hoke Grenn, five years younger than Junty, had no eyes for Cory. He couldn't stop staring at the strange men with enormous brown eyes like dollops of chocolate. Somehow he also managed to store away three platefuls of nearly everything on the table—which was a great deal.

There was meat, fried and tasting like pork and looking more like mutton; terrips, both mashed and diced and pan-fried: they were pale yellow but were not sweet and tasted like what they were: local potatoes. There were two other vegetables, including the staple red beans called gralthi, cooked long until they were soft and mushy. And biscuits, and the thick, almost-white gravy that the Grenns dumped liberally all over everything on their plates, including the biscuits.

Besaneh Grenn, who was a year younger than Hoke, spent most of her meal gazing longingly at Cory's clothing. And, of course, at Berneson, the only possible magnet for any romantic thoughts.

Galeaneh said hardly a word, merely making certain everyone had enough of everything and striving to prevent her children from harassing the otherworld people overmuch with their questions. She had instructed them to call her Gally, and she wore a faded figured dress with elbow-length sleeves. Its hem fell to just below her knees, the least attractive of all lengths, surely. Her hair, shot through with threads of gray, and was worn in an ancient Earth-style called the ponytail.

Her sons wore the same sleeveless coveralls of heavy gray cloth as their father, but with identical shirts of pale yellow, a nubby, grainy cloth that Cory liked. Besaneh, too, wore one of the coveralls, but with a print blouse beneath. All wore boots outside, rising to midcalf; all went barefoot indoors. Thinking that the custom might possibly be a religious one, Rinegar made certain that he and his companions left their soft boots just within the door.

"Well," Rinegar was saying, "there's Earth, and all the planets settled by Earth—maybe yours was, a long, long time ago. And there's Azul, and its planets. The Azuli aren't like us. They are only one race: all very white, like clouds, with only a little hair and what there is of that is so white it's almost invisible. Otherwise they're humanoid. Two legs, two arms; mammals."

Junn Grenn glanced at Berneson, and Berneson grinned. "Aren't there any people like me on Home, Junn?" The Grenns' word for their planet was Bor, which meant Home, naturally enough.

Junn, Junty, Hoke, and Besaneh all shook their heads, simultaneously, big noses slicing the air before their faces.

"None," Junn said. "Not that anyone knows about, anyhow. Oh, there are some sort-of golden people we call yellow, and most of the world seems to be people who're more brown and less red than we are. But no, Berneson, I've never seen anyone so pale before."

"I love your *hair*," his daughter said, and Berneson grinned at Besaneh. There wasn't a sign of a curl in her glossy black hair, bobbed quite short with a cute little pointed sideburns that would look funny, waving in a high wind. "It's so curly."

"Well, that's a better word than kinky," Berneson said.

"But . . . *war*," Hoke said, using the word of the strangers; his language held no such word or concept. "People . . . ending each other's lives. Why?"

Ringar sighed, pushing a piece of fat away from his meat.

"Because we are the only two races in the universe, or at least all we've found so far," he said. "And we've become rivals. We've tried to get along, and I'm sure the Azuli tried too."

(Cory, her lower lip out, was shaking her head.)

"At first there were just incidents," Ringar went on, "here and there and elsewhere. Then worse ones. Azuli 'pirates,' if you can call them that, attacked our ships in space. And our government blamed Azul in general, the government, rather than the individual Azuli outlaws. The same thing happened in reverse, too, and the Azuli accused us of doing it deliberately, as a sort of revenge."

"It was a lie!" Cory snapped.

"That's chauvinism," Ringar said quietly, "and it's an unworthy—emotion."

"We studied—"

"I was around when it happened," Ringar reminded her, "and you studied your lessons in wartime. You don't think humans are going to tell their children the enemy isn't all bad, do you?"

Junn Grenn was frowning. "But she isn't a child, certainly. How long has this—*vwar* continued?"

Ringar sighed, looking at his plate. "Eighteen years."

He heard their gasps, knew they were staring. He glanced around, then bent again to his plate. It was hard enough to "explain" war to people who knew the concept. How to try to explain it to those whose language didn't even contain the word?

"What would you do," Berneson asked, "if someone came in here while you were in the fields, Junn, and . . . burned your barn?"

Junty grinned. "No one would do *that!*"

"If someone did? Or stole a worg?"

"Uh—well, I would go to town and tell the magistrate," Junn, senior, said. "But no one would do that."

"And *if* someone did, and you *did* go the magistrate and tell him—then what?"

Junn shrugged. "The same if someone stole an animal or a piece of harness or a hammer or a discer," he said, "or anything else that belonged to someone else. He'd be put on display in the town square, with his name on a sign above his head and what he had done. Everybody who passed by would see him."

The offworlders noticed shivers among the Grenns.

"And—and then? What if he did it again?" Rinegar asked.

They all stared at him, Junn and Gally and Junty and Besaneh and Hoke. And stared, as though he were insane.

"No one ever has," Junn Grenn said to his plate. He swiftly developed a great interest in his gravy-buried biscuit halves, and Rinegar narrowed his eyes, watching him. At last he nodded.

"Will you go back?" Besaneh asked, of Cory.

"We can't," Cory told her. "I mean you don't have space travel, do you. A way to get off Home?"

Junty chuckled, received a look from both his parents that was almost vicious. He apologized instantly. Rinegar nodded.

"No-o-o-o," Besaneh said, wagging her head.

"You mean you *can't* leave?" Hoke asked suddenly; his voice piped a bit.

"We can't leave your *bor*," Rinegar said quietly, "and return to our *bor*, unless someone comes for us." He looked around. "And . . . and I hope for your sakes no one does."

Cory and Berneson looked at him, but he did not return their gazes. He was noticing. Now it was Hoke who'd recieved one of those Looks from both his parents and his siblings, and he appeared more than embarrassed. He apologized, and his voice was so low it did not pipe at all.

Rinegar accepted a piece of yellow-orange fruit from the little wicker basket Gally passed. He examined the fruit, a flago, and asked abruptly: "You'd never ask us what we will do here, would you?" And he immediately bit into the flago's white pulp.

No; they gave him that questioning-his-sanity look again.

"I thought not. Well, we'll find something. This is good, Bernie; try one. None of us knows anything about farming, I'm afraid. But there must be something we can do here."

"Maybe in Veern," Besaneh said.

"Veern?"

"The town," Junn said. "Stores, and a bank and things. I'm sure you can get work there. No trouble at all. Or the carnival, as I said."

"But you'll stay here tonight, won't you?" Besaneh asked, eyeing Cory's purple tunic.

"We—"

"We have room," Junn said in his quiet, seemingly imperturbable voice, "and of course you must stay with us. I am sorry if I've failed to mention it. You are tired?"

"It's been a long day," Rinegar said, wondering how long it *had* been; there were no "days" on a spaceship.

His watch persisted in telling him what time it was, and how long he had been awake, but its face and numerals were meaningless on the world called Bor; Home.

"Hoke and Junty will just double up tonight," Junn said. "And Beşaneh, you will sleep with your mother—"

"Excuse me," Rinegar said, "but that surely isn't necessary . . ."

"Couldn't—couldn't Cory just sleep with me?" Besaneh asked, and her mother and father looked mildly shocked. Then they noticed that Cory was not at all offended.

Junn said, "Well . . ."

"Of course," Cory said.

"Oh, wonderful!" Besaneh cried, her big dark eyes seeming to sparkle, "and I have *two* nightshirts, too! See, Mother, aren't you glad I made that other one?"

After that the Borean girl could hardly wait for the meal to end, so she could clear the table. Never having cleared a table, Cory watched and got in the way. Berneson and Rinegar and Junn Grenn were discovering the same strange fact: they had little to talk about. They could not discuss the crops and the worgs and the weather with him, and neither wanted to put him through an endless question-and-answer session. They were more alien to these strange hyper-polite people, despite physical appearances, than the little white Azuli were to the children of far Earth.

They answered a few questions back and forth, in no great detail, and eventually they went to bed. Rinegar and Berneson shared the smallish—and eminently comfortable—straw-ticked mattress Hoke had had to abandon, while Cory and Besaneh ascended to the loft.

There Corisande answered excited questions from the other girl until she fell asleep in the middle of one.

In the morning they were awakened by the Grenns, who were obviously trying to be quiet in deference to their guests but who, after all, had to be up and cracking; it was nearly daylight. They visited the little building out back, one by one, and washed their faces in the pan of water on the back porch, avoiding the plank Gally warned them about with a reproachful glance at her husband.

"Oh yes," Junn said. "Hoke, fix that plank today. Do a good job, now."

Hoke nodded without a word, looking neither happy or un-.

"What has to be done today, Junn?" Ringar asked.

"The darf's still standing in the field next to the one I was working yesterday. Has to be cut: winter forage for the cows." (Not cows, of course, *worgs*. But they *were* cows, while the offworlders were uncertain as yet what *darf* might be. Alfalfa? Rye? Wheat?)

"I'd like to come along later," Ringar said. "I can't say that I'll be much help, but I will try to stay out of the way."

Junn gazed at him thoughtfully, then nodded, his eyes crinkling as he laughed. "Yes! Very good," as though Ringar had made a fine joke.

Maybe I did, Ringar thought, *to such mild people. Maybe I did. Most likely I just proved what a good guy I am. It isn't hard, when I can see into his mind, 'hear' his apprehensions.*

"Suppose . . . suppose I walk out later," he told Junn. "We do have to talk, you know, the three of us I mean."

"Of course."

"Have to decide what they're going to *do,*" Hoke

piped, and caught another Look. Without sighing or making a face, he looked instantly down.

"It's a pre-industrial-revolution world, isn't it?" Cory asked, as the three of them walked along the bank of the little stream across the field and down the long grassy hill behind the barn.

"I'm not sure," Rinegar said. "They do have machinery. The pump in the kitchen, for instance, attached to the cistern—a crude sort of faucet, you see, with a hand pump to replace an automatic one, building up the water pressure. It works. We didn't think to ask, did we?"

Berneson snorted, wearing an exasperated face. "You two dummies must be blind. That was an authentic Ford's Folly under the little roof-thing beside the house."

"A what?"

"Was it, Bernie?" Rinegar had stopped. "An automobile."

Berneson nodded. "About 1910 style, or something like that, I'd say. Maybe 1920; I'm not a history expert. It's hard enough to keep those early centuries straight, without having to pick out specific decades. Anyhow, before the middle of the twentieth century."

"A gasoline automobile, you mean?" Cory cried, startled and horrified.

"I don't know. I didn't examine it. But I'm sure it was an automobile. They may still call it a horseless carriage, of course. It wasn't new, I'll tell you that."

"Don't be too shocked, Cory," Rinegar said with a little smile. "We started the same way."

"But they're *poison!*"

"I really doubt that the pollution from the few low horsepower engines they *probably* have so far will shorten your life, Cory," Rinegar told her. "But that moves them up a good half-century, just having an automobile and some sort of engine."

Berneson shook his head. "I'll bet their history is a lot longer than Earth's already," he said, frowning and absently toying with his heavy forelock. "People who don't even know what war *is!*"

"That's what I wanted to talk about," Rinegar said, squatting and watching the water giggle by a few feet down the bank, sparkling and gleaming here and there where it was struck by the sun sneaking through the trees. He picked up a smooth little pebble and plopped it into the lazy water. The pebble lay there; the stream flowed gently on, without taking notice of the disturbance. *Like this planet,* he thought. *Like these people.*

"These people have codes," he said, "or a code. It's obvious that the worst thing on Home is *embarrass-ment.* You must not ask another person his business, or say anything that might embarrass him in the least way. Think about it: punishment for what I assume are the very few crimes here is . . . very light. But there are apparently no repeaters."

"So Junn says."

"Umm, but he wasn't lying. Although, suff, he doesn't know everything there is to know. Anyhow, that's why the children got those *looks,* every time they said or asked something that might have given us the least bit of mental anguish. It's as if the motto were *Step Not On Another's Toes.*"

"Motto and prime commandment," Berneson added.

Rinegar nodded. *"Verboten;* taboo: Apologize at once! Junn and Galeaneh just wouldn't do it, and the children, of course, must be taught. Junty's the oldest—you didn't notice him making a slip or getting one of those looks."

"He was too busy eyeballing our girl here," Berneson said, and when she jerked her head up she saw that he was smiling easily. She looked down. "Hm . . ." he said, narrowing his eyes. "People like these would certainly be easy to . . . to take advantage of, wouldn't they?"

"That's why you said what you said," Cory cried, looking at Ringear. "About hoping for their sakes that no one finds us."

He nodded, staring down the bank into the water. "Yes. Either the Earth Union or the Azuli League. Either one. These people would be like . . . children, to them." He sighed, looking around. "What a lovely pastoral world."

"Lovely," Berneson said. "Lovely, What are we going to *do on* this lovely pastoral world?"

"Raise gralthi," Cory giggled, then realized the seriousness of the question and frowned.

"Well, if they have pumps and automobiles," Berneson said, "I'll bet someone has invented an airplane or is working on the first one right now. It's just a step from that to space travel, isn't it?"

"About a century," Ringear singed without looking at him. "That long at least for them to get anywhere past their own system. But these people—" He shook his head. "Look, you saw a what? Would you call it a crude automobile."

"About a T-model, Jake. I know a little about old cars. They—interest me."

"Nice hobby," Cory said very quietly, "on Home."

"Yes," Ringear said, staring at the water and frowning, "on Earth that car was about two decades after the first one, as I remember. I could be off a decade or two. Anyhow, *here* the automobile might have been invented a hundred years ago."

They stared at him. Slowly, Berneson began nodding. "Yeah . . ." he breathed, barely audible. "No war . . . placid people . . . easygoing, slow—it's as if man developed on this planet without challenge or difficulty, without having to develop survival skills— defensive skills that *our* ancestors used for offense, attack. Without the inventions that come out of war and then are used otherwise." He shook his head. "Good lord, they could be hundreds of years away from space travel."

"Hundreds? Bernie . . . when people curb their curiosity, when showing curiosity is a sort of crime because of their own social system, why should they *ever* try to leave their planet?"

"We're—stuck here," Cory said, staring at nothing with wide sad eyes, "for—forever."

They were all silent for a time, while the devitalized little stream chuckled on.

"Unless a Union ship happens to find Home and, for some reason, set down here. And even then, *if* we are anywhere near. Remember that. We might be a hundred miles away and a spaceship could land here and leave and we might hear about it a month or two later."

Berneson was gazing up at the sky through the interlaced leaves of the trees growing along the brook. He sucked up a long deep breath, let it out very slowly.

"The Azuli," he said, "have just as good a chance of discovering Home and landing here as the Union has!"

Cory didn't feel embarrassed by her shudder; she noticed that Rinegar, too, shivered. And she could not remember any other time that Berneson's voice had held a quaver.

She wondered fleetingly at his hushed words, and

wondered, too, if in addition to teleportation he had the Power of prophecy.

5

When the rain came up, threatening the fresh-cut darf, the three aliens to Home considered demonstrating their psi Powers. Or at least tney considered using Corisande's telekinetic ability to move the crop from field to barn. (Berneson's suggestion that he gather an armload, teeport to the barn, drop it, and teeport back for another handful, was rejected as being ridiculous. Berneson was grinning, anyhow. He couldn't take seriously a rainstorm on a crop on a pastoral planet.)

They decided against letting the Grenns, and Home, know about their Powers just yet. Instead, the three pitched in to help Junn and his family load the hay into his cloar-drawn wagon. Junn creaked up and down the field riding a cloar-drawn rake, a long collection of semi-circular wires that resembled an openwork tunnel. The side-delivery rake left the darf in long rows, with room between them for the wagon. Thus, with pitchforks, they were able to load the wagon from both sides at once.

They did not quite beat the rain, but when it began there was only one wagonload left to bring in. The rest of the fresh fodder was in the loft. They spread out the final lot to allow it to dry. Damp-stored hay not only rotted, it became so hot within its piles as to be a fire hazard.

They learned a few answers: yes, there were trains. Steam locomotives. Junn wasn't certain when they

had been invented, but his daughter advised proudly
that the first working steam engine had been invented
two hundred and six years ago. The trains were about
a hundred and forty years old and were being converted to the new engines—as they wore out. The new
engine utilized the combustion of petroleum fumes, of
course. And yes, the primitive automobile outside was
in working order: it was only four years old, and
hardly driven, and one of the proudest Grenn posses-
sions.

"How long ago," Rinegar asked quietly, looking apprehensive, "was the automobile invented?"

"You people sure are interested in time," Gally
Grenn said, smiling. Then her smile faded as she
doubtless wondered if she might have given offense.
Step Not On Another's Toes!

"The first horseless buggy," Besaneh said, for she
was the best student among the Grenns, "was invented
by Hork Norbeek, eighty-nine years ago. Ours is a
Norbeek Mark II."

The three Earthsiders looked at each other. The
gasoline car was eighty-nine years old here on Home,
and the Model T outside was a Mark *two!* Norbeek
and successors, apparently, had seen fit to make one
major change in their machine in eighty-nine years!

On Earth, Krebs had put his gasoline-engine Pan-
hard on the road in 1894, and changes in body and
mechanics had been legion, year after year. Within a
century, the machine the staid Britannica persisted in
calling the "motor car" was so ubiquitous in the
United States that it had been responsible for thousands and thousands of deaths annually, both from
accidents at speeds up to and in excess of 160 kph and
from its ghastly hydrocarbon and sulfuric acid pollutants. And the country had been involved in a great
nationwide argument as to whether it should build

jet-engine transport aircraft that would *cruise* faster than the speed of sound.

On Home, after eighty-nine years, the Grenns were proud of their "brand-new" Model T. And there was no air travel at all.

"What about a similar vehicle to pull your plow or your rake and so on?" Rinegar asked after a shocked silence.

Junn nodded. "Yes, I've heard of such. Some big farmers're using them, I understand. Maybe there'll be one at the fair. I can't see much use for the things, though. They make a horrible noise, they need gasoline and oil and have to be kept inside, and what good would they be in winter? No, that sort of thing isn't for the small farmer. They'll never replace the cloar," he said, referring to the gray-and-red Borean "horse."

No, Corisande thought, *tractors will never replace horses on this complacent planet—not for about a thousand years, anyhow! These people probably went as long as Earth's entire history without even inventing the wheel!*

"I can hardly wait till tomorrow," Hoke said, bouncing up and down in his chair. "The fair, the fair!"

"You people will come with us, of course," Galeaneh said. "Better let me wash your clothes out tonight, with ours." She hesitated. "Unless—"

"Unless, Mother?" Junn prompted.

"Well, unless they'd rather just borrow some clothes from us," Gally said.

"Mother!" Besaneh was horrified. "And not wear these bee*yoo*tiful things of theirs?"

"I think that would be a very good idea, Gally and thanks," Rinegar said, ignoring Berneson's and Corisande's stares. "I'm sure we'd rather just enjoy the fair without being so different." He glanced at Berneson. *"He's* going to be different enough," Rinegar smiled, although Berneson already had a little tan. Rinegar had warned him about sunburn. "Anyhow, once we get to town we can buy—"

He trailed off. Buy new clothing. Home-style? With what?

Not only were the Earthsiders on a strange and comparatively undeveloped planet, among people so shockingly uncurious that they made curiosity taboo, but they had no money and no trades—none that would be valuable on Bor, at least. Sure, they had their Powers—but demonstrating such abilities might get them a cell and/or a witch trial.

Rinegar sighed, and he was still sighing and looking disconsolate next morning when he stood watching Junn crank up the Norbeek (Mark II!). There seemed no way they could all get into the car, and Rinegar said so.

"We can get's far as the Meerkins'," Junn said, "somehow or nother. There's only Preek Meerkin and his son, and they'n take some of us in *their* Norbeek."

"Is—is there just the one kind of car?" Corisande asked her built-in translation system bringing out the word "car" as "automatic wagon."

"Sure," Junty said, grinning at her. "How many does anybody need? Oh, there are several companies, is that what you mean? Yes, of course. Most of us call all of them Norbeeks, and most of us who have one buy a genuine Norbeek anyhow. They were the first, after all."

And thus the oldest, Cory thought, *and that makes them better.*

Somehow they all crowded into and onto the high car perched on its skinny little tires, and it but-butted and backfired its way down the dusty drive and out onto the road, which was of fine gravel—and potholes. Perhaps two miles later they had a flat tire, and rather than fix it Junn merely replaced it with the spare. This was a simple matter: Junty and Berneson and Rinegar held up one side of the emptied machine while Junn worked. Then they re-boarded and bumped along another half-mile to the Meerkin place.

"How do you know they haven't already left?" Berneson asked, grunting under the weight of Hoke (seated on his knees) and wearing Junty's hipbone in the side of his thigh. They could at least have placed Besaneh or Cory beside him; their hips were a little better padded then Junty's!

Junn Grenn chuckled. "Preek Meerkin's never got anyplace within an hour of on time in his life," he said. "They had to hold up his wife's funeral almost an hour, four years ago. And we're early, anyhow. I doubt they've even finished breakfast yet."

And he was right. The Meerkins were obviously not ready to leave when the Grenn Norbeek rolled up before the two-story frame house. Preek's face was whiskery, and, sharply prompted by his son, he had decided to remove the growth in honor of the fair. Meerkin was short, barrel-chested, and coming on for being barrel-bellied too. His black hair was well threaded with white, so as to resemble something painted by an artist with an overused brush. His son was six feet tall, well-built, and quite handsome, with a ferociously black mustache.

There was considerable discussion, but both Cory and Besaneh allowed they'd be happy to wait and ride in with the Meerkins. Berneson opted to accompany them, which was not to Besaneh's distaste at all. The others drove on to the Tri-County Fair and Carnival, a great collection of varicolored tents and sawdust and trampled grass and people, sprawling over several acres a mile or so this side of Veern.

(Berneson wore a hat and a neckscarf, grumbling

but agreeing that his face, fairer than any other on
this planet, was better shaded against the sun—and at
least shadowed.)

Rinegar waited for him and Corisande by the gate,
watching the steady inflow of the people of Home.

No, not Home: Bor. They spoke only the local language here, and all three of them had agreed that calling a patently alien planet "Home" was . . . hurtful.
Worse than uncomfortable. It reminded Cory and
Rinegar of Earth; Berneson of Mars. Both were far
and far from Bor and its sun, both in terms of distance—millions of miles—and of time—centuries
ahead.

*I see a lot that's mighty similar to the old fairs on
Earth,* Rinegar mused, as a six-person family passed
him to enter the gate. They had arrived in a two-cloar
wagon, which hired attendants would look after. *And
a lot that's different. The animal . . . the color of
some of the fruits and vegetables they're bringing in
. . . and the unimaginative clothing. Berneson would
call this a far cry from civilization . . .* An ephemeral
little frown touched his face.

He stood there over an hour, unbored. At last the
Meerkin car arrived, backfiring scandalously and
wearing the flat tire as a spare. He had managed to
speed his father along, Preek's son Preeky said, but
they'd had a flat, and the elder Meerkin had never got
around to fixing the spare from last time. So they'd
patched it, pumped it up, and now he would take it
and the Grenns' spare into town to be fixed. And a
bright-eyed Besaneh would accompany him.

The three Earthsiders, reunited, strolled into the
fairgrounds at last.

"I see a source of income," Rinegar said with a
grin. Following the direction of his nod, the others

saw a weight-guessing booth, presided over by a man in a bright yellow shirt and matching baseball-style cap. He grinned and winked as they approached, sizing them up.

"I'll bet you a sprole I can guess *your* weight," Rinegar said. "Within one pound."

The man cocked his head, studying him, and pulled at his down-flowing mustache. "Never had anybody approach me *that* way before, cousin. Hmm . . . you ever work in a carnival?"

"I have not," Rinegar said, tapping his lips as he'd seen the others do; it was akin to saying "I swear," on Bor, an indication of absolute veracity. "Never. I've never guessed a weight before, come to think."

"What makes you think you can guess mine?"

Rinegar shrugged. "I feel lucky today." He took a deep breath, smiling and looking around, glancing at the sunny sky. "It's a great day, isn't it? Wonderful day for a fair!"

"Suppose we say that I'll take that bet," the man said, "but just in case, I get to guess all three of yours, too."

Rinegar grinned, glancing at the sign: weights guessed for ten sprolets or three for a quarter. He'd bet a sprole, a hundred sprolets. He agreed. "Do you know your weight?" he asked.

The man nodded, smiling. "I weighted not fifteen minutes ago, with my pockets empty, checking the scales," he said, and of course he remembered it then, and instantly Rinegar had his weight.

"Were you dressed?"

The man laughed. "Cautious, aren't you, now I've accepted your rash challenge! Yes, of course I was dressed; you think I'd stand out here and strip?" He removed a few items from his pockets. "And now I assure you my pockets are empty. Well?"

Ringar gave him his precise weight. The man's jaw dropped.

"How'd you do that?"

Ringar shrugged. "I read your mind," he smiled. The man didn't laugh, but merely shook his head: not likely! And with another sigh he reached into his cashbox and counted out four quarter-sproles. He smiled, picking up one of them.

"This one I keep," he said, "for your weights," and they laughed, and he came within his allowed three pounds of each of their weights and thus they had earned four quarters and spent one. They moved away. The guesser gazed thoughtfully after them for a moment, but then directed his attentions and chanting, cajoling voice at a little clot of people merging from one of the vegetable-display tents.

"Hardly fair," Corisande muttered.

Ringar nodded regretfully. "True, but we have to earn some money, and this is my—trade. I'll repay him as soon as I can."

"Well, I can't think of any way *I* can—" Cory broke off, gazing with large blue eyes across the midway. She smiled, clapped her hands, and hurried through the crowd. Berneson and Ringar exchanged a look and followed.

Precisely the same sort of booth had existed in fairs on Earth centuries ago, and may well have existed time out of mind, when Caesar and Cyrus roamed the Earth. First a wooden counter with a smiling couple behind it, and a collection of hard leather-covered spheres like baseballs. Then, some ten meters away, a little wooden box on the ground, forming a platform. On it rested a pyramid of silver-painted "bottles," which of course were metal. And there was a rack of prizes.

"It's money I need, cousin," Corisande told the couple behind the counter.

He shook his head, smiling. "It's not money you'll be getting here, snippet." He waved a hand. "We've got every sort of prize you can covet, though, and we'll hand them to you cheerfully—provided you knock over the bottles! Are you so confident? What's a girl know about—"

"Never mind making fun of my sex," she said sharply. "What's the object of your game?"

"Knock a bottle off and win another three throws," the woman said; she was round-faced, round-bodied, and tired-looking behind the eyes. "Knock two off and win a prize from the first row. Knock all three *off the platform* and win a prize from the second row." She smiled "Do it twice and take your choice of the BIG prizes from the third row!"

"It"s money I need," Cory muttered, but she placed her quarter on the counter. She was handed a sprolet and a fiver and three "baseballs." They were called flagors, after the fruit. She turned to smile at her companions, then completed her windup.

The first ball missed cleanly, thumping into the canvas back of the booth.

"Going to have to do better than that, snippet!"

"Just getting the range, snip," Cory told him, and launched another ball. It sent the topmost bottle spinning off the others.

"The little lady wins a PRIZE," the booth's proprietor cried, attracting all the attention he could. "A prize, just for knocking a little bottle off with the big ball! And she has another thr—"

He broke off. Cory's third throw sent the flagor precisely into the space between the remaining two bottles. The space was not large enough to allow the ball to pass through, and both bottles shot from the plat-

form in opposite directions. Slowly the man turned to
stare at her.

"You're . . . very good, cousin," he said.

"Good enough to be addressed as a human being
rather than as 'snippet,' hm, cousin?" She smiled at
him. "Keep the prize—I'll take three more balls. I
have three coming free, right?"

"Right," the round woman told her, and placed
them on the counter. Cory glanced around to discover
that she now had a small audience.

"Bet she can't do it again," a voice behind her said,
and another replied, "Bet she can! Put your sprole
where your mouth is!"

"Wh—what . . . put my . . . ah yes. Yes! I will
wager you a sprole, then. Say you sure don't get much
sun, do you cousin?"

Grinning, Cory picked off the bottom right bottle
with her first throw, spilling both it and the top one
onto the sawdust. She exerted no mind-control on her
second cast, and was surprised at how close the ball
came. But Bernie had a one-sprole bet, and he did not
possess one sprole. With visions of his being jailed,
she directed the third ball with her polite-Power
again, and sent the third bottle tumbling.

There was a great deal of excited and astonished
noise behind her, and a couple of gasps directly in
front of her.

"All right, cousin, here's your sprole—that girl's a
miracle!"

"I doubt that," Berneson's voice said, "but I'll bet
she's good enough to do it again—two of the bottles,
at least."

"You what?" There was a pause while the Borean
considered. Then: "If she knocks off none or three, I
win? Taken?"

"Double or nothing?" Bernie's voice asked, and a

frowning Cory heard the slow agreement, and then someone else offered to bet, and she sighed and started her windup. She threw without mind control but trying to hit the bottles, and she missed them by a half-meter. The second throw went low and struck the box with a loud *thop* sound, rattling the bottles and incidentally proclaiming that the box they sat on was hollow. But the metal "bottles" were undisturbed. She had to do *something*, and so the third time she carefully mind-directed the ball into the neck of the bottle forming the right side of the little pyramid. It and the top bottle fell, struck the box, and rolled to the ground.

The booth's proprietor and his wife were almost smiling.

"That earns me three more," Cory said, holding out her hand.

"But you've already—"

"Give the little girl her three flagors," a voice spoke up beside her. "She earned them just as she said."

Cory turned a bright smile on the tall man there. He looked more City than most of the other fairgoers, in snugly fitted blue trousers and dark blue overtunic. A pale green scarf was knotted about his neck, and his boots were well polished. His mustache looked as if he clipped it every morning before breakfast.

"Thank you, cousin," she said, holding her hand out for the balls without looking at the booth's proprietor. "I think I was just about to need a champion."

"You're the best hurler I've seen since Sprencore," he said, returning her smile and leaning on the counter. "Do you play flag?"

Sprencore, she knew, was a major city, considerably distant. *Flag* simply meant "sphere." Borean baseball?

She shook her head, blond hair whipping across the back of the print blouse she'd borrowed from Besaneh. "I never have," she said.

"You should. You might well be the first girl ever in the game—if they'd allow that! Well, don't let me hold you back."

So, excited, delighted, flattered—and anxious to show off—she sent the first ball flying to knock all three bottles off the little platform with a great clinking clatter. This time there was a great deal more reaction, all about. The man and wife running the booth scowled; the man beside Cory gasped; applause and excited exclamations arose behind her.

"What's the prize for knocking them all off with one throw?" her champion asked.

"None. There isn't a special prize, I mean. Just—"

"What I really need," Cory said, "is money, not prizes."

"Hm. And you've won—how many, Frell?"

"That's . . . three of the big ones," the counterman said.

"Four!" A new voice called, and Cory turned to beam at a chunky boy with an angry face. He grinned at her, then frowned again, looking past her into the booth. "Four, and you know it."

"You forgot," Cory told the man called Frell. "It is four, remember?" *There,* she thought, *I'm giving you a chance,* snip. *Better admit it or you may be robbed!*

"Four, yes," Mrs. Frell said, and her husband pretended to ponder, at last nodding. "Oh yes," he said. "I'm sorry—she's been here so long I lost track. You're keeping a lot of people away from the booth, cousin."

"NO SHE ISN'T!" the chunky boy bellowed from behind her, and Cory chuckled. Now she had two champions. "WE'RE WATCHING!"

"I really think you should give the others a chance," the tunicked man behind her said. "Those prizes are worth about a sprole each, wholesale. Really, yes. The big ones, not the trinkets."

Suff, she thought, *stuffed animals and ugly vases and junk!*

"But I'll tell you what," he went on. "You do it one more time and I'll give you five sproles and buy your lunch into the bargain. I'd like to talk with you."

She studied his face, then nodded. "All right," she said. "I'm Cory."

"Coory? Cory? Unusual. . . . I am Laramen Skeal. It's your throw, Cousin Cory."

Frell was at the back of the tent, gathering the flagors. Cory glanced around and shivered; she'd drawn a tremendous crowd. Borean faces gazed at her from all sides, and they were all shapes and sizes and ages. The midway was a bright flower of fair-day colors, all across, and all the eyes were on.

She threw, struck the box. She threw, mind-sped the ball just above the top bottle. Frell smiled. She smiled back, threw without paying much attention, and mind-guided the flagor into the base of the pyramid of bottles. There was a loud gonging sound—and the ball rebounded.

Cory blinked. Astonishment gave way to anger as she heard the mutters behind her. Shaking, she was on the point of picking up the ball with her mind and crashing it into the bottles when there was another concerted gasp and voices rose anew. She looked up to see a tall man at the back of the tent, wearing a farmer's coverall over a plain shirt of pale tan, with an off-white scarf about his neck and a slouch hat shading his face. She recognized the clothing Berneson had chosen to minimize his fair skin, unusual both on Bor and on Earth.

He bent, reaching down behind the box supporting the bottles, and held something high in the air.

"The box is open at the back," he called, "and this is a *magnet!* The bottles are metal. Perhaps you'll allow her to throw once more, friend—with a chance of winning?" He was talking to Frell.

Frell started angrily toward him, but the man beside Cory called out. "Frell! Stop right there! I told you in Larl there'd be no more of that, and I thought you'd thrown away your magnet." He drew paper and pencil from his tunic pocket and scribbled quickly in the squiggly Borean script. "Here, Frell. Give this to Paymaster, and get off the lot. I don't have cheating the customers in my carnival."

His face cloudy and dark-scowling as a day on Quar, Frell said absolutely nothing. He twitched the paper from Laramen Skeal's hand, spun to shoot an angry scowl at Berneson, and walked straight to the rear of the tent. Her lip trembling, his fat wife followed. They departed and the flap dropped back in place.

"Here you are," Berneson called, and he tossed the ball to Skeal. Then he too turned and raised the back of the tent and was gone.

"I'd swear that man just appeared there out of thin air," someone behind Cory said.

"Sure is a pale one," someone else said. "But let's don't start manufacturing miracles—that girl's one, all by herself, and one miracle's enough, any day!"

"Your throw," Skeal said, smiling with a little bow, and he handed Cory the ball.

"It took a nasty blow," she said. "I think I'll use one of these others, Cousin Skeal."

Deciding to build the drama, she missed with her first throw, cleared off right and top bottle with the second, and barely tumbled the third one with her final cast.

"Very good," Skeal smiled, and handed her five one-sprole bills. "And there's your money, Cory."

"You own the whole carnival?"

"My brother and I, yes. I manage it. And I now lack a manager for the flagor booth. You prefer money to prizes; would you like to earn some?"

Corisande smiled, tilting her head. She waved a hand. "Running this?"

"For the rest of the morning at least, yes. I think this will be a very busy booth for a while. And if business slacks off you could always give a demonstration, couldn't you?"

She nodded, smiling sunnily, and he named a figure, payment if she worked through the lunch hour. She nodded and went around to enter the tent from the back. Taking the cashbox, Skeal left her three sproles change in coins and ten in bills. He pocketed the rest. She smiled. There was certainly no reason he should entrust the morning's receipts to a total stranger, she realized.

Skeal stood about for awhile, and he was right: business was very good indeed. Every male in the audience she'd raised was anxious to best the snippet. None did, but sprolets jingled in, and then sproles, and when she looked up at the series of screams from the Wonder Maze, Skeal was hurrying off that way.

As Cory started to the rear of the tent-booth a moment later to retrieve the thrown flagors, the flap rose and Berneson stepped in. He dropped the flap behind him. "Hi. Need some help?"

"I sure do," she gasped. "These people are running my legs off, and my back's already sore from picking up balls and bottles. Where've you been since you lined your pockets betting on me?"

He was squatting, picking up flagors and tossing them forward to the counter. "Oh, having a little fun."

She squatted behind him, filling her little coin apron with balls. Suddenly her head came up to stare at him, and she gasped.

"Bernie! Oh no! You teeported in and out of the Wonder Maze!"

He chuckled. "I teeported in and out of that place several times," he said blithely. "People go in there to be *scared*, right? Well, today the've been getting their money's worth."

"Oh, *Bernie!* Why can't you do something *worth-while?* This is work—but it's fun."

"So," he said sulkily, "is scaring people."

"Bernie, please don't—"

"Hooey! You going to take *all day* back there? I'm going to knock those bottles clear out through the back of the tent!"

And Cory had to hurry back to the counter to collect the impatient customer's sprolet and lay out three more flagors. Berneson departed grinning.

6

"Take a card, any card," the tall thin man with the pointed black beard called, and Rinegar paused at the edge of the smallish crowd. He watched. One of the onlookers reluctantly laid down a fiver, a half-sprolet, and slipped a card out of the deck the bearded man extended. The red-lettered yellow sign above his head proclaimed him Thertoono the Great: "thertoono" was the Borean approximate of "Marvello."

Ringar watched, squinting his eyes and staring at the back of the card drawer's head. When the farmer looked at his choice, he sent a momentary flash from his mind—without, of course, knowing it. Ringar was able to pick it up: the card was the seven of buckles. Folding his arms, Ringar waited while the farmer was told to slip the card back in, anywhere in the deck, after which Thertoono shuffled, three times. He began slapping the cards down on his little counter. Suddenly he paused, went back one card, and held up the seven of buckles.

"I almost missed that time!" he cried.

"That's not much," a woman near Ringar muttered. "My son Heerd can do card tricks."

And the others seemed to agree; Thertoono had had little enough crowd to begin with, and that was drifting raggedly away. He waved his cards and called out his cajoling come-on, without takers. Ringar moved up to the counter.

"One fiver to take a card," Thertoono told him, smiling, "and if I guess wrong you win double. Two to one, my man!

"Call me cousin," Ringar said quietly. "It's not so condescending. These farmers don't want to be called My Man by a bearded slicker."

"Wha—what?"

"How many times have you misguessed this morning?"

Thertoono's smile returned. "Not once—uh, cousin; but you never know, you never know. Only the Sun Himself knows the answers to all things, you know," he said, obviously quoting.

Ringar sighed. "Thertoono, how long have you been doing this?"

"Listen, cousin, who are you anyhow?"

"Cousin, you have to miss every now and then, to keep the customers interested and coming. Here—here's a fiver, and I don't want your sprolet. Now for steen's sake, *lose!*"

"Lose! Why, I—"

"Thertoono, lose, and not so loud. Come on, now. Here, I'll take this one."

Ringear withdrew a card and held it high, turning to show it to the few people behind him without letting Thertoono see it. He turned and slipped it back into the deck.

"Lose once, Thertoono," he said. The bearded man stared at him, frowning, then slowly raised an eyebrow. He was shuffling the cards automatically. *I think he's got it,* Ringear thought.

Negative. Ringear had withdrawn the three of straps; Thertoono hold up the three of straps. One person applauded.

Ringear turned "Bet he can't do it twice," he told the pitiful little gaggle of onlookers. "This time I'm not going to show *anybody* my card!"

He slapped down another fiver, took a card, stared at the nine of buckles a moment, and replaced it in the deck. The magician shuffled once, twice, three times, and began snapping the cards off the deck and slapping them onto the counter with a flourish. He put down the nine of buckles, then another card, then frowned, turned his head on one side, and picked up the last card. *Nothing like a little suspense,* Ringear mused. Then, *You idiot!* Thertoono had held up the nine, Ringear's card.

"The nine of buckles!"

"Wrong!" Ringear cried with great jubilation.

Thertoono stared at him. *"Wrong!"*

Ringear nodded solemnly. "Wrong, Thertoono. He

can be beaten," he said, turning with a smile.

"Hooey—the magician lost, the magician lost!"

"Mother, can I try it with the cards?"

"Here's my fiver, Cousin Thertoono. Let me just draw one of those cards. Hooey—shuffle them up, come on. Beat him, eh?" The red-faced man grinned at Rinegar. "I will too. We'll break him up, won't we!"

"I'm next, next right behind you," a pre-teen boy cried.

Rinegar gazed meaningfully at Thertoono, who was staring back while his facile hands shuffled the cards, on full automatic.

"You see, cousin?"

Slowly Thertoono took his eyes from Rinegar, focused them on the red-faced man. He held out the cards with a jerk of his arms.

"Choose a card, cousin," he said. "Any card at all. Thertoono never misses twice."

"A sprole says you do!" someone shouted.

"I am not allowed to carry on private wagers," Thertoono said, with a sad little smile.

My good deed for the day, Rinegar thought, walking on.

Attracted by screams from within, he moved over to the Tunnel of Love. It appeared to be exactly what it had been on Earth: a fun-place for noisy youngsters, romantic husbands and wives, and occasional young couples, the girl smiling at the ground while her swain paid their fare and helped her into one of the little six-person boats.

But now one little boy was yelling bloody murder and his older companion was crying and shivering, and a stern-faced man was helping a fainting woman from his boat.

"What's the matter here; what happened?" The ticket seller deserted his booth to hurry to the excited persons, who could be very bad indeed for his business.

The man looked stormily at him. "Listen, I'm going to make sure no one rides in your place any more, scaper! If we'd wanted to be scared half out of our wits we'd have gone through the Wonder Maze."

"But—"

"Get away before I—" The man did not finish the sentence, but for the first time Rinegar had seen a Borean bordering on violence, and had almost heard a threat. He went swiftly to the man and his limp companion.

"She's just fainted," he said. "What happened in there, cousin?"

"You a physician?"

"No no, but I know a little. She'll be fine." He straightened up. "Here, now—move back a little and let her have some air; you know about that." He turned back. "What happened?"

"It wasn't her imagination, I'll tell you that! There were the four of us in the boat, those two boys in the front seat and me and my wife in the nextun. The back seat was *empty*, empty! But all of a sudden the whole boat rocked, and a hand came up on my wife's shoulder and a man laughed. She screamed, and I started to turn, trying to grab his hand, and—I swear," he said, tapping his lips, "he was there—and he *vanished*."

Berneson, Rinegar thought angrily. *He's probably put this place out of business for the day, and he could've given someone a heart attack*. He swung to the ride's proprietor.

"I'm going in there," he said. "They think they saw something."

"Saw something? What—wait, wait . . . Say, who are you?"

Rinegar was already stepping over the low board fence and hurrying along the little walkway beside the water.

"Hooey!" the carnival employee called, but Rinegar was into the tunnel, taking the little needle-pistol from the spacepod out of his pocket. He took five steps in the darkness, striving to see, when suddenly an empty boat went by—they were automatic, riding a cable— and a slouched-hatted man *appeared* in it.

"All right Bernie, stop it! You'll ruin this man's business, you idiot, and a woman's fainted out there. What if she's in shock?"

Berneson vanished—

—and reappeared on the walkway and swung at Rinegar. Rinegar jerked back, maintaining a precarious balance—and heard the pistol *ploop* into the water. Berneson disappeared again.

A voice accosted Rinegar from behind: "Who were you talking to?"

He backed from the tunnel, edging along the walkway, and turned to face the man who operated the boat rides. "I don't know," he said, "but that fellow was right. Someone was in there, scaring people. He ran away—maybe the others saw him." He knew better.

"Oh no! He'll ruin my business!"

"Possibly," Rinegar said, just as angrily. *And lost us our only weapon too,* he thought. "Keep trying. Wait— someone just grabbed your cashbox!"

The man spun. "Who? Where?"

Rinegar began to sweep the crowd with his eyes; no one seemed to be moving any faster than anyone else. That girl looked excited—no, she was trying to decide whether to accompany her pushy date through the Tunnel of Love. That man—yes! Rinegar caught the excited thought from the fat man's mind. He had the cashbox. Rinegar moved away from the ride's proprietor, made a swift semicircle through the crowd, and accosted the fat man head on. He jerked to a frightened stop, his chins quivering jellylike.

"Give the man back his cashbox, cousin," Rinegar said.

"Wha—what—I don't have . . . what're you talking about?"

"I'm talking about the receipts from the Tunnel of Love, friend, and your hand inside that big coat of yours. It's a little too much coat to be wearing on such a nice day, now isn't it?"

The man threw down the box and ran on fat legs, his dark coat swirling around him.

Busy Jake, Rinegar mused. *I could always make a living as a security guard on this planet. Hm . . . so there are thieves here.* For some reason the thought was almost cheering. It made Bor a little less alien, a little more like home. *How sad, that I feel better on an alien planet because it has thieves,* he reflected, handing the box to the grateful proprietor of the Tunnel of Love.

"What'll I *do?*" the man asked plaintively, as though Rinegar could provide the answer to *all* his problems. Already this dead-faced man had frightened off the frightener and retrieved a stolen cashbox!

Rinegar smiled. "Just stand around awhile and look pleasant, cousin. I imagine you'll have some business in a few minutes; it's a big crowd, and that man's wife is all right." He waved a hand and walked on, observing the fair crowd, primarily ruralites, and both listening and mind-listening to them. He caught no hint of violence or larceny.

Good. The needler was lost and it would be totally ruined even if he could somehow fish it out of the dark waters of the tunnel.

Maybe a thief on Bor is a mental deficient, he mused sadly, unable not to make the comparison with his own people and their long history of stealing and slaying. *Maybe a thief is,* everywhere—*and all us earthsiders are psychotics!*

After wandering through a large tent displaying new machinery, woefully primitive, he decided to return, walking up the other side of the midway, to see how the magician was faring. When he met Besaneh with Preeky Meerkin, he recommended the Tunnel of Love. Predictably, the girl looked down and Preeky grinned nervously.

"Well . . . since you recommend it so highly, Cousin Jake—"

"I do," Ringer said. "But be sure to take the last seat. No others—wait to get the last one." Just in case Berneson was fool enough to continue his japery, Ringer wasn't anxious to send friends into fear. He walked on, pausing to watch an archery shoot and thinking of Corisande, when he heard a shout louder than the many around him. He turned, feeling himself in another mind, and looked around.

At a table on the edge of the dining pavilion sat Thertoono the Not-so Great, with a thin woman about his age. Ringer nodded, Thertoono beckoned, and Ringer ambled over.

"Sit down and let me buy you a cup of drim," Thertoono said. The beans of the drimple tree made a passable coffee on Bor, with a faintly cola flavor. "I won't vow that I *like* you, cousin, but you certainly helped my business."

"Tell me about it," Ringer said, bobbing his head to the woman Thertoono introduced as his wife. He sat down.

Thertoono told him about it: he had won several times, then lost just as a large group was passing, and he'd had plenty of business ever since. Enough to enable him to close his booth to enjoy a sandwich and a drim with his (hatchet-faced) wife, Ethneh.

"Now answer the question you didn't answer before," Rinegar said, nodding his thanks to the girl who brought him his mug of steamy drim. "How long have you been with the carnival?"

After giving him a strange look, examining his eyes, the waitress departed. Rinegar found himself being scanned just as closely by Thertoono.

"You're a strange man," the card-magician said thoughtfully. "You've known great sadness, haven't you? You smile, but your eyes don't. And the lines in your face—"

"Theery!"

"I'm sorry, I'm sorry," he said, patting his wife's arm but speaking to Rinegar. "Uh—we just started yesterday. This is my first time at this, I mean. I was, uh, running a dart throw, before."

A sensitive, Rinegar thought. *Not unusual among people in any sort of entertainment business, and especially those who wind up in "magic" or illusions.*

"Think of your name," Rinegar said, and after a moment, "Theerd Smisel."

"Why, how did you know *that?* You're in the business, aren't you? That's how you knew—"

Rinegar shook his head. "Do you know your weight? Think of it," And a moment later he told the bearded man his weight.

"That's—exactly right," Thertoono said, leaning forward.

"Um. Theery, let's raise your price to a sprolet and raise your audience and fame at the same time. With half for me, mind."

"What? What—how?"

We're stuck here, Rinegar was thinking. *These people have not heard of either Earth or Azul, and they don't even have air flight, much less space travel. We're stuck here . . . forever. I said my Power was the only trade I knew, but it's dangerous. Well, it isn't in a carnival! Everyone will think I'm just a very clever trickster.*

"Let me explain," he told Thertoono. "D'you have your cards with you?"

7

Corisande tried merely to avoid telling the truth, but found that she was forced to lie to Laramen Skeal. He wasn't the same sort of person as the Grenns, and she couldn't tell him she was from a world he couldn't even see in the sky on a dark night, or that she had a well-developed mental Power known variously as telekinesis or psi or poltergeism; that she was a psier, a telek, a poltie.

She was forced to answer his questions when he bought her lunch as he'd promised. He had returned to the booth just after noon, bringing a man with him to relieve Cory at the flagor throw. They had both been astonished at the amount of money Cory had taken in. The crowd around the booth was less than anxious to lose the pretty girl who never missed; but she called out, she had to eat, after all! They had laughed.

She told Skeal she wasn't from around here, that she hadn't any parents, that she was with her uncle

Jake and her cousin Bernie and that she wasn't certain
how she could throw so well.

And she wasn't, really. Some on Earth had one of
the Powers and some did not. All children were tested
and trained, practically from birth, but only one in
thousands developed the Power as she had, as Ringear
and Berneson had also.

"Well, right now," she answered another question,
"we're staying with the Grenns. They're . . . friends
of Uncle Jake's."

"Who are the Grenns?"

She shrugged, smiling. "Friends of Uncle Jake's.
They have a farm a few miles from here."

Skeal leaned back, studying her with highly intelligent brown eyes like dark spots set well back in his
face.

"I'd like to talk with Uncle Jake," he said. "You
have a real . . . talent." He added, smiling, "Or something. You and I could both make some money with
it. You're show business."

"He's around here someplace," she said uncer-
tainly.

He paid, she thanked him, and they walked along
the midway, sidestepping people, running into people,
being run into. Against the background bee-buzz of
the fair-goers' conversation, the interminable shouting
and wheedling of the barkers swelled and receded as
Cory and Skeal passed the various booths.

Abruptly Skeal stopped. He glanced at her. "Here,
Cory—try this."

She looked over at the dart throw. "You mean really try?"

"Of course. Can you do this sort of thing accurate-
ly, too, or is it just ball throwing you're so good at?"

She threw three darts and broke three balloons. The

booth's operator looked perplexedly and a bit unhappily from her to his boss.

"It's all right, Sper. She doesn't want a prize, do you, Cory?"

"Uh—just a cane," she said in a small voice, and Sper and Skeal laughed and she walked on, carrying a bright red cane with a gold-and-purple top.

They stopped again, and she tossed five rings. She missed with the third—deliberately. But the other four settled over their targets, causing a minor furor and exerting a superb effect on that booth's business.

"If I'd known about this," she said, "I wouldn't have bothered throwing flagors!"

He laughed, then raised his head, frowning. "Hello, what's all this? Let's just see what's on the other side of this crowd, Cory."

They had difficulty pushing through the crowd before the garish red-and-yellow sign, but they reached the third rank after a few minutes and a few angry looks.

"But above all do not show the card to my associate," the bearded man was saying. "That's right; now let everyone else see it." He laughed. "Not me, of course! Fine; now if you'll just slip it back into the deck, anywhere."

He shuffled three times, while Cory gazed at this associate. He sat there on the little platform too; a middle-aged man in undistinguished attire—small-farmer's Sunday best, if there was a Sunday on Bor—and with a very sad face, almost exanimate. Not calm or placid, like that of most Boreans she'd seen. Genuinely sad, stricken, marked with the lines of agony.

"Rinegar," she murmured. It was as though she were seeing him for the first time. *I called him a cow-*

ard. A coward! A man who had spent years, nearly all the years of the war, working in Intelligence with his wife, often within Azuli area, in constant danger. A man who had been wounded, who had reesed—felt and seen in his mind—his wife's awful death by torture, and who still had returned with the information he'd been sent to get. *And I called him a coward,* she thought. She felt small and young and callous and stupid—and conscience-stricken.

Now he sat on a carnival platform on an alien planet, a planet peopled not with enemies, but with inhabitants who were, to him, incredibly primitive. Beside him on the platform was a yellow sign with red lettering: *Thertoono the Great.*

Thertoono was slapping down cards so that everyone up front could see them. Ringar was watching, with a great look of concentration on his face.

"Stop!" he intoned with drama. "That is the card." And Thertoono held it up with a flourish and the crowd oohed and aahed and applauded. They were not gambling; they were paying money to see a performance, and very little money at that.

He in't concentrating, Cory thought. *It's just an act. He's pretending. He got the card from the mind of the man who drew it, minutes ago. I guess he doesn't dare not look at the cards. That would be too much!*

"Who the—I never saw that man before," Skeal muttered.

"That's my uncle."

Laramen Skeal looked down at her. "Your . . . uncle," he said quietly. And after a moment: "What's your *cousin* do, girl?"

When the Grenns went home that evening, their new friends remained behind—and Ringar had scrupulously repaid the weight guesser. Early in the morning, just before sunup, Berneson teeported out to the Grenns', in half-kilometer "jumps." He was sitting on their porch when they arose.

"How—how'd you get here?"

Berneson smiled. "I've brought back your clothes, and we are in your debt. We'd like our clothes . . . and here are some passes to the fair, any time this week. Come again."

Junn nodded, smiling, while Gally hurried inside to fetch the strange clothing of the three strangers.

"I haven't told them what you told me," Junn said. "The more I thought about it, the more I felt I shouldn't. Are you—are you really from—" he waved a hand at the sky. "From another world? Up there?"

"Yes."

"Well, I don't think I'll tell anyone. You're nice people. No use getting everyone excited, is there? Or to wondering about you."

"No."

"How'd you really get out here this morning?"

"I—came."

"Flew?"

"Not exactly."

"Something like?"

"Something like, Junn."

Junn nodded insouciantly. "I don't know if it matters, Bernie, but I think I'll just not tell anybody you're from another world."

"I think that's a good idea," Berneson told him. "We really shouldn't have told you."

"Um. How'll you get back? Will people see you?"

Berneson had to admit it to himself: *Stupid!* He hadn't thought of that. He sighed, mentally kicking himself. "Yes. I'll have to w—"

"I'll have Junty hitch a cloar to the wagon," Junn said. "You'n ride back that way, and he'n spend some more time in town. We need some things. Come on in and have some breakfast, Bernie."

"Thanks," Berneson said, smiling even while he frowned inwardly. It was a strange feeling. Had he ever had a friend? There hadn't been much opportunity, being a psi and getting all that attention, adulation really—after the bigotry he'd felt in early childhood, because he was so fair of skin—and growing more arrogant by the day. Especially at the front in the war, when he was so important and knew it. But Junn was—a friend.

"Is Bernie going to eat with us?" Hoke asked.

"Yes," Junn told him.

"Oh good, good! Junty, Besny—*Bernie's* here and he's going to *eat* with us!" The boy turned back to his father and the lightly tanned man from Mars.

"Dad *said* you three could get a job with the carnival, didn't he, didn't he?"

Bernie had to laugh, and something made his hand go and ruffle the boy's black mop of hair. "He did indeed," he said. "Your father's a mighty smart man, Hoke, and—a friend."

Part 2

The Boreans

8

After two months with the carnival, traveling from town to town and living in the carnival-owned trailer vacated by the man Skeal had fired, the three had refined their individual acts considerably.

Corisande could not only hit any target with anything she threw, she was also able to throw far. Her status rose. She became one of the perfomers, rather than merely the operator of a booth who attracted business by staging demonstrations. It was a simple matter for her to launch a spear at a target entirely too distant for her strength, then to pick up the spear in flight, with her mind. She then carried it on to thunk it into the target by mind alone. Her feats were incredible, but after all she was with a carnival, and people expected the incredible.

She heeded Rinegar's warnings. She could have "thrown" the spear, or the ball or a dart or, for the matter of that, a needle, any distance up to a half-kilometer. Which would have been patently impossible. The spectators ("marks;" Berneson introduced the word to Bor) would not have believed such a feat. Perhaps they didn't believe as it was, but accepted the likelihood of some sort of trickery. But as long as the performers' feats remained somewhere within the realm of possibility, the audience believed—because its individual members *wanted* to believe in the incredible.

But Skeal would have known, and so would others with the carnival. And they'd have known there was something more than "mere" incredibility involved. For a slim sixteen-year-old girl to send a javelin, or any missile at all, a half-kilometer through the air would have been *impossible*. And the impossible made people nervous—and worse.

"Incredible, *sí*," Rinegar said. "Impossible, no!"

He, meanwhile, had also become a performer in the evening shows for which the spectators paid an extra sprole. First he was a mentalist, with Berneson as assistant. Then he added magic to the act: it was not at all difficult for him to "make" the other man vanish! At the proper moment, Bernie simply teeported himself into their locked trailer. There he sat watching the clock, and after the proper interval he teleported back onstage. To resounding applause.

"But the applause is for *you*," he complained.

"Can't be helped, Bernie," Rinegar sighed, glancing at Cory. At first he had seen her as a child of sixteen, and he had felt kinship with the other man. But now it was obvious that pure-sensation Bernie was the child of the trio. And Cory was maturing, daily.

"The one thing we can*not* do is let them know we really do have Powers. You can't put on a demonstration of teleportation, Bernie, any more than I dare pick any person in the audience and start giving a complete rundown on him from his thoughts."

Corisande turned, eyebrows lifted in curiosity. "How could you do that, Jake?"

"Ask him questions. If I ask you your birth date, the answer jumps into your mind whether you want it to or not. I immediately know when you were born, whether you tell me or not—hey, you're about to have a birthday!"

"You'd better start saying 'hooey' instead of 'hey,'" she warned, but she was smiling. "I see, though. You instruct someone in the audience not to say a word and to avoid thinking of the answers to the questions you ask. Immediately he gets excited and starts broadcasting, right? Then you ask him one question after another, and write down the answers or call them out a moment later."

"Right," he said, shrugging. "Easiest thing in the world, for a reeser. But also dangerous. People would begin to realize that we have Powers. First they'd call them super*human,* and then someone would think super*natural,* and we'd start getting into trouble. Investigations, tests, security, red tape, fear of us."

"Or prison or the Borean equivalent of burning at the stake."

"Yes, yes, and we're talking about *Jake* again," Berneson said, slamming a hand down on the built-in counter that was their dining table. "Jake—Jake, Rinegar the Great. And Corisande the Incredible. But whoever heard of whatsisname, Rinegar the Great's assistant? Well, I'm *tired* of being a shadow, a magician's assistant!"

Rinegar pulled his brows down, furrowing his forehead. "Well then, think of an act you can do without letting them know you're teeporting, Bernie, and that's that: you're in business too."

"Yes yes, oh shuff. A teeport act without teeporting. Right." Berneson's voice was tight as his lips and his frown was one of petulant anger, not concern as Rinegar's was. "Meanwhile I'm expendable! Skeal might decide to economize and lay me off or put me in a booth, taking sprolets and handing out darts. Or

suppose he decides your act needs what all Earthside
magic shows had: a little more glamor? A little sexual
attraction, a good-looking dolly to stand around
smiling, wearing a sequined swimsuit or whatever.
Then where am *I?*"

"That's not going to happen, Bernie," the older
man told him. "Look, this has come up before. I
won't allow it to happen."

Berneson thrust his face out, stretching his neck to
resemble an angry bull-worg. "That's just it! I don't
want it to be *you* who's taking care of *me,* Jake. I
don't need taking care of."

"One of these days," Cory said, sighing, "we're
going to run out of things to bicker about—and what
are we going to do then?"

The two men stared at her. Ringear thoughtfully,
Berneson with anger. Then he left the trailer, petu-
lantly.

A few days later all of them had come down with a
slight fever and nasty sore throats. The prospect of
having contracted some disease or viral infection on
such a primitive planet terrified them, and their bick-
ering worsened. But their throats cleared up within a
few days, leaving them a little hoarse for a few days
more, and after that they were very careful of their
health. Meanwhile Corisande had her Idea:

"Bernie! Look away a moment. Turn your back."

"Suppose you just stop telling me what to do, brat!"

"Oh Ber-nie," she said, in the tone and manner she
had learned could sometimes overcome his childish
petulance, at least long enough to get out of a tight
spot and onto a new subject.

He gazed at her a moment longer, then heaved one
of his high-shouldered, melodramatic sighs and turned
his back to her.

"Thank you, Bernie. Now turn around and look."

He turned. She was standing just as before, wearing the floppy white sweater and the tight whipcords she'd dyed purple. (She was after all in show biz, she said, and she'd begun to do and wear things she knew she could get away with; things people both condoned and expected of performers.) But now she had both hands behind her back.

"What am I holding behind my back, Bernie?"

"What? Ask Jake! I'm no reeser. Play your silly games with The Great Rinegar-r-r-r-r, the marvel of the age!"

"Come on, Bernie," she smiled. "You can find out what's behind my back. You have a way, too."

He cocked his head at her. Started to blast her with more angry words. Reconsidered. Vanished—

—reappeared behind her, whirled to face her back, smiled, vanished again—

—to reappear where he had been, facing her from a few feet away. "You're holding your hairbrush," he said, "in your left hand."

She laughed, genuine delighted merriment like a mountain stream bubbling over smooth-washed stones. "Right! Right, Baffling Berneson, and that's your *act!* You can see through solid objects!"

Jake raised a hand to finger the gray-shot Vandyke beard he had raised, as befitting Rinegar the Great. He narrowed his eyes.

"Bernie . . . she's right. All we have to do is work out the details—and figure a way to disguise your vanishing and reappearing. Hm . . . all you need do is call for a volunteer from the audience, having him go behind a curtain and do something. A dance step, pick his ear, anything. And, ah—" he grinned at Corisande—"Baffling Berneson tells exactly what he was doing."

Berneson eased slowly into a straight-backed chair.

"We'd have to have a booth—some hokum, getting people to check it out, make sure it's perfectly normal, no false bottom or mirrors or anything. When the mark goes behind the curtain, I step into the booth. Then—"

"There's a partition behind the curtain," Cory put in excitedly. "You teeport in on the other side of it and peep at the mark through a little hole there—"

"—And pop right back into the booth onstage, and out," Bernie said, staring at the wall and licking his lips, "so the audience doesn't have time to miss me, even to *think* I might have left the booth onstage!"

"Someone comes onstage and turns his back to your booth—pretty girls are best—and makes some little sign with her fingers or holds something in her hand. Meanwhile you pop out of the booth, take a look at her from behind the curtain, and teleport right back into the booth and walk out!" Rinegar said, just as excitedly. "Again, the *timing's* important—just as fast as you can make it! And you tell her what she just did. That way the audience knows you're right, because they saw her."

Corisande was practically dancing. "Then you ask for a volunteer, and let the audience agree or veto the volunteer, and you ask that one to do something really complicated with his hands!"

"Bernie," Rinegar called, slapping the other man on the shoulder and squeezing, "you're in business! All we need is a finish!"

But the finish was a simple matter. As the conclusion of his act, the Man with the X-Ray Eyes merely bowed to his applauding audience—and vanished.

"It's stupid and it's childish!" Rinegar snapped. "There's no reason for it, either. Cory, *Cory!* A big part of your act's success is that you're a sweet-faced teen-aged girl. Mothers in the audience wish you were theirs. Girls in the audience identify with you. Young males and fathers wish you were their sister or daughter. Why spoil it?"

She stamped her foot. "I'm not a child! I'm *tired* of being a sweetyfaced teen-ager! I'm seventeen years old and I've been in a war! I'm a woman and I've got a body and they know it."

"Right," Rinegar said, nodding exasperatedly. "They all know it. So why scream it, why cheapen yourself by wearing—that?"

She clapped her hands to her hips, glanced down at herself, and looked up at him with eyes of ice reflecting fire. "And what's wrong with *'that'?*"

Rinegar sighed. "You're a performer, a star attraction. You have a talent and a popular act. Why dress like a showgirl, a hoofer in some chorus line for an audience of drooling males? Look at you—I've seen more clothes in steam rooms! You—oh, no!"

Her eyes had grown misty, then tears had spilled over to rush glistening down her cheeks. Now she burst into noisy sobbing.

"You just want me to be a little girl! You don't want me to be a woman and you don't want me to be attractive—you just don't want me to be as popular as you and your act!" she wailed, making herself look even more ridiculous in her self-designed new outfit: a bright yellow bra, sparkling with Borean sequins; low-slung purple briefs; broad-meshed black hose that disappeared beneath the briefs; and spike-heeled shoes consisting mainly of straps.

I said too much too soon, Rinegar thought, watching her with his teeth set in his lower lip and his hands fisted. *When will any of us ever learn control,*

*learn to be people and stop pecking at each other like
vicious chickens? The outfit is wrong for her, wrong
. . . but I could have thought a little and found a better way to tell her! If only we could act like friends
rather than . . . family.*

"We—we'll s-see what B-Bernie says when he
comes in, you mean old man!" she cried, collapsing—
but not forgetting to flounce—into a chair and pillowing
her head on the arms she folded on the breakfast
counter.

Without intending to, Rinegar caught a flash of
thought from her over-emoting brain: *Bernie! He's
young, he'll like it! He'll love it, I know he will! And
he'll stop thinking of me as a silly brat, too. I'm as
pretty and sexy as all those farm girls he's got
drooling over him!*

Bernie, Rinegar thought. *All he's been doing lately
is making a play for the local girls wherever we stop.
That's why he demanded his own trailer—and got it,
now his act's so popular. He'll get us into trouble yet.
He's also highly likely to come in here and tell her she
looks marvelous.*

He was standing there, chewing his lip as he stared
at her long slim legs, when the door was jerked open
and Berneson stepped into the trailer.

"Say, I—" He broke off, staring at the faceless girl
bent over the table. "Oops! Jake, you old dog! I didn't
realize you'd picked up a little something from
downtown. Sorry, nothing important; I'll come back
later. Bro-therrr!" And rather than departing as he'd
come, he vanished—to reappear, Rinegar assumed,
back in his own trailer, which he himself called the
Girl Trap.

Cory had ceased her weeping, just like that—which
made Rinegar suspect just how much realism there'd

been in her brokenhearted weeping and how good an actress she was. But there were tears on her cheeks and in her reddened eyes when she looked up, betrayed. She sniffled.

"You—winked at him," she accused. "You managed to send a thought or two, rather than just picking brains as always. He couldn't have meant that! No one could mistake *me* for—"

"Say-y-y," he said slowly, "you—"

"I'm going to *kill* myself! No one likes me, no one loves me. Everyone thinks I'm a child and when I dress like a woman everybody thinks I'm just a—"

"Wait a minute," Rinegar said, as if she hadn't uttered a word. He'd heard, all right. But he had hit upon a solution, he hoped. A compromise. "Cory? You know . . . you have *beautiful* legs. I think you're right: if you've got it, flaunt it. Yes! Call attention to your legs—how clever of you! Listen, I've got a suggestion you might consider, to make the most of your best feature. Why don't you have some sort of tunic made, Cory—mid-thigh length, something dark. And wear boots—your own boots, the black-and-silver ones. You might try to find a pair of white ones, too. Listen, you'll—"

She was gazing bright-eyed at him, her expression rapt. She tried very hard to smile, and she was almost succeeding. Soon, she did.

The boy with the slingshot grinned, drew it back as far as he could, and let fly his stone. He was as good as he'd bragged, his younger brother saw: the stone flew straight and true to bounce off the flank of the cloar hitched to the carny wagon. The animal jerked, reared, emitted its bleating cry, and lunged forward. The wagon lurched after, and both the man and the trunk he held tumbled off its back.

"Run!" Hork yelled, and he spun and ran, still clutching his slingshot. Their parents were over that way, and thus he raced across in front of the frenzied Borean horse. It swerved, already breaking into a gallop. The wagon trundled loudly after it.

Hork's younger brother froze, trembling, then started to run—after his brother, naturally. Blind with fright and the singleminded desire to get somewhere else as quickly as possible, he didn't even seem to notice the plunging cloar. Just as blind, jerked out of its snooze by the sharp sting at its flank and now totally disoriented, the animal was rushing toward him. Someone screamed, then someone else. Not the boy; it was as if he saw nothing.

Then, with the cloar centimeters away, a man appeared as if from nowhere and lunged against the boy. Both of them fell, rolling and flailing. The cloar's hoofs hurled sawdust and dirt over them as it galloped past. A locally hired tent-staker grasped the side of the wagon as it trundled by, and swung himself aboard. In less than a minute he had the panicky cloar under control.

"You saved his life! You saved that boy's life!"

"Look—it's the Man with the X-Ray Eyes!"

"It's Berneson!"

"Look, look, it's *him,* and he saved that little boy's life!"

Emerging from her trailer in response to the clamor, Cory didn't bother to check the trunk Berneson had been loading for her. She ran to where he and the wailing boy were picking themselves up.

"Bernie! Are you all right?"

"Shuff," he said, nodding and glancing nervously around at the swiftly growing crowd.

"You're a *hero*, Ber-nie! Are you all right, little boy?"

The boy replied by yelling for his mama, a fat woman who was pushing her way through the jabbering onlookers. Behind her came a man as skinny as she was fat, his big bony hand clamped around the wrist of a huge-eyed Hork.

Bernie ignored her thanks. He bent swiftly to jerk the slingshot from Hork's hand and wave it before the boy's father's face.

"This little criminal used this to bounce a rock off that cloar, *cousin,* and the animal nearly killed his brother! *I* could have been killed—now get off this lot and take that brat with you!"

"Now just a minute—"

"You get that little beast out of here or I'll take you both to the magistrate!"

Blinking, the man collected his wife and sons and departed. Averting their glances, the onlookers backed from their hero. The crowd drifted away, almost in silence.

"Oh Ber-nie," Cory said softly. You're a *hero*. You shouldn't—"

"I'm not interested in being a hero," he snapped "It was pure reflex. I saw him, I saw the cloar was going to trample the little idiot, and I was just *there*. Scummy parents who can't control their slimy brats—I could have been killed!"

"But Bernie—"

"For steen's sake, Cory, *shut up!*" And Berneson stalked off. "I should have let him die," he muttered. "Would've served him and his idiot parents right."

"It's against his concept of himself," Rinegar told Corisande a few hours later, as their trailer moved along in the caravan, heading from Sprencore to Slee-spoken for a week-long engagement at the District Fair and Agricultural Exhibition.

"You mean you think he *wants* to be bad?"

"He'd like to, yes. We're all rejects, Cory. Bernie more so than we—remember his color and the chip on his shoulder. It's the same reason he was tubed and sent back from the front, because of all his nutty tricks. For some reason he wants *negative* attention. Being a hero doesn't thrill him. I think he'd much, much rather be a villain."

She sighed, watching one of her new mid-thigh length tunics sway and swing on its hanger as the trailer rattled along. "That's—that's awful, Jake. That makes me . . . sometimes Bernie makes me feel just *old!*"

"I know." He nodded, peering out at a herd of worgs, not one of which bothered to look up at the brightly colored caravan passing their pasture. "I know exactly what you mean, Cory. The term 'child' doesn't have a lot to do with how long a person's lived."

"What if he—if he decides to do something really bad, Jake? Sort of to make up for being a hero? Oh, Jake! What're we going to *do* with him?"

"Jake still having those dreams, Cory?"

She nodded, pushing her food around her plate. "He just can't forget, Bernie. Sometimes the sounds he makes when he's dreaming about it wake me up, right through the door to the other room—gasping and pleading and muttering about *her.* He wakes up with a headache, because he was wounded while they were torturing her, you know. Then he drinks some more. He's drinking too much, Bernie. I mean, I think he might be."

He shook his head, glancing around. "He's not old, and any woman here would love to have him notice her." He sighed. "But he never even looks at a woman."

"I don't think he looks at anybody, Bernie, not really. People stare at him though, and he knows it. Those *eyes* of his!"

Bernie interrupted the meal they were having on the midway to scribble his autograph on the program proffered by a girl. He handed it back with a smile and she left, reluctantly, smiling in return. Bernie turned back to Corisande.

"Fellaneh's crazy about him, did you know that?"

"Fel—the aerialist? She's young enough to be his *daughter,* Bernie!"

He nodded, smiling. "Some men bring out the mother in women and some bring out the daughter in them. She knows he's fifty, and she's twenty-three. But she'd let go at twenty meters up if she thought he'd be standing there to catch her."

"And he ignores women! He ignores everybody, or almost. He just doesn't seem to want to have anything to do with people. He—"

"He doesn't want to form emotional attachments," Berneson said, twisting his face exaggeratedly as he pronounced the old psychiatric phrase. "He's scared of them."

That's true of you, too, Cory thought abruptly, realizing she'd had another of her insights. *But you handle it differently; you're trying to be the Don Juan of Bor, to prove whatever it is you think you have to prove!*

"Oh, Ber-nie! What're we going to *do* with him?"

9

The big Sleespoken Fair was held in late fall, and it ended the fair season and the season of Skeal's carnival as well. It was also, as it turned out, the end of three of its acts: Corisande the Incredible, Rinegar the Great, and Baffling Berneson: the Man with the X-Ray Eyes.

Two days after the carnival arrived in Sleespoken, the wind came up, strong and cold from the west, and Rinegar looked up sharply at the screams; both the audible ones and those keening in his mind.

The tent pole, he realized at first glance. *It's going to* fall! *It's—*

Horrified and helpless, he clenched his hands and stared at the great center pole of the main tent. It had not been sunk deeply enough in the loamy soil outside Sleespoken, not deeply enough for this pre-winter wind, anyhow. It was already beyond the wavering stage. He saw its top move leftward—and then he saw it *stop.* It continued to waver, but it remained there, defying wind and gravity. He glanced around, frowning, then strode to seize the megaphone from the barker's trembling hand.

"Clear the tent! CLEAR THE TENT! THE POLE IS NOT FALLING, BUT WE WILL HAVE TO BRACE IT. PLEASE DON'T PANIC, BUT PLEASE CLEAR THE TENT. THERE'S PLENTY OF TIME —PLEASE DON'T PANIC!"

Even as he shouted the words that emerged as a bellow from the other end of the megaphone, they seemed familiar. He remembered:

REMAIN CALM . . . THERE IS NO RUSH; RE-PEAT, NO NEED TO RUSH. THERE ARE SPACE-BOATS FOR EVERYONE. . . .

And I did panic. And I did again, just now. What am I doing, standing here telling everyone to be calm? Me!

But he knew why. Because someone had to. *She* couldn't handle it all alone. She was testing her strength even now. The pole might break free at any moment. Someone else had to act, had to help, had to tell that milling gaggle of screamies to get out of here.

I'm the only one who knows, he thought, staring at her.

A slim tall girl with lots of blond hair flowing and tumbling down the back of her tunic. Her white-booted feet were firmly planted in the sawdust, perhaps twenty meters from the tent's center pole. Her head was tilted back as she gazed at the trembling pole.

Cory. Holding the pole upright by mind alone, saving ten or a score a hundred lives, by mind alone. A slender teen-ager, looking very fragile as Rinegar gazed at her stiff back, defying the wind, fighting it with her poltie mind.

Several people were injured, but whatever it was that had kept the pole from falling until a few seconds after the last fair-goer was outside had saved many lives. Some said it was a miracle, and a university professor worked very hard to postulate a mathematical answer for the pole's sudden refusal to be blown over. He was trying to explain by logic something that had no logical explanation, not unless one knew about psi Powers. The religionists came off better with their explanations. Church attendance in Sleespoken leaped upward, and so did the collection the following Sunday, the fair's last day.

Cory was very tired afterward, and after that she was silent, devitalized; introspective and profoundly thoughtful.

"They're praying to you, in a way," Rinegar said. "It's a shame we can't tell them, Cory. I'm the only one who knows you're the miracle."

"It doesn't matter," she said abstractedly, and the shutters of her face closed again and she returned to her thinking.

On the fourth day after the carnival's arrival in Sleespoken she said, "You know, we really could do a lot more with our Powers. . . ."

"Shuff!" Berneson agreed with a swift bob of his head. "We'd make the best bank-robbing team of all time, on *any* planet!"

The sunny expression melted like wax from her face.

On the fifth day after their arrival in Sleespoken, Rinegar's turn came.

By then they had learned that Boreans did kill Boreans. Not often, and seldom in passion. Calculatedly, for express purposes; and the thought that wafted to Rinegar from his audience was like a foul aroma.

Two overweight men sat side by side. There was little difference in their ages; both were in their forties, to judge by their hair and the lines they wore in slabby faces.

They were brothers. And the younger was going to kill the elder. They had inherited a great deal of property, and the younger sibling Taige felt that he lived in his elder brother's shadow.

Rinegar did not think twice about it. He interrupted

his own performance to stride down through the audience, passing Corisande, who had come to watch his show before dressing for her own. Rinegar signed to her with his eyes. It was enough. She frowned, but nodded almost imperceptibly.

He came to a halt before the two men.

"I wish you good evening, Lamen and Ijssel Taige. And I must tell you, Ijssel Taige, that your brother Lamen plans to kill you."

The shocked gasp came not only from the brothers Taige but from everyone in that portion of the audience able to hear Rinegar's words.

He knew at once that he had acted precipitately. But how was one to handle such a situation? Another way, he was sure, as he stood there before them; some other way, after careful thought and consideration. Not just a loud-mouthed public confrontation. *Rinegar, you idiot,* he told himself.

But the shock proved beneficial to the chosen victim. Even as he was starting to turn his jowly slab of face to his younger brother, looking both shocked and questioning, Lamen was scrambling up from his seat. He thrust a hand into his stylish overwrapped tunic, whipped it out again. A knife glinted in the spotlight that had followed, laggardly, Rinegar's unexpected descent into his audience.

"You've ruined it!" Lamen Taige shouted, almost screaming, seeming close to tears. "I've planned so carefully, and now you've *ruined* it, magicker! But you'll not stop me!" And he raised the knife on high, to stab as an inexperienced man does, rather than to thrust.

He was right. Rinegar did not stop him. Corisande did. Rinegar was sure of that, watching the astounded expression clamp over Lamen's face like a mask, watching the upraised arm twitch and tremble, seemingly held by invisible strings.

You're right, Corisande, Rinegar thought. *We do make a fine and formidable team. What we could do!*

He had, after all, spent sixteen years in the war with Azul, and he had been trained. His left hand streaked out stiff-fingered into the man's gut, and as Lamen Taige *whoofed* and started to double up, Rinegar's other hand fell onto the back of his neck, edge-on. Already folding, on his way down, the would-be killer kept straight on dropping, but with added momentum. He fell with a potato sack thump-soggy noise, and his knife clattered off one chair rung, then another.

Lamen did not get up.

Rinegar and Ijssel Taige stared at each other, and the small dark eyes in the slabby face were bright as fever. For a moment neither heard the rising crescendo of the audience's reaction.

"He . . . really was going to . . . kill me," Ijssel Taige said. Although Rinegar saw the man's thick lips move, he did not hear his words. But he "heard" him, just the same.

Rinegar nodded. "Yes. He really was."

Lamen was carted off by the miserably confounded magistrate and his assistant, both looking as if they had little notion what to do; after all, an attempted killing, and *violence!*

The elder Taige and Rinegar talked long together, over a bottle of friendship. The following afternoon he was back, and this time his conversation was with Cory and Bernie as well as the man Ijssel already called Jake. They made their agreement.

Crowds were very good indeed the final night of the District Fair and Agricultural Exhibition outside Sleespoken. There was a Standing Room Only sign out for Rinegar the Great, and he received a long ovation even before he began his performance.

And the carnival was over, and Laramen Skeal bade be well to the three who had been with him so brief a time, and had done so much for his receipts. Yes, Rinegar promised him. If at all possible, they would make guest appearances for Skeal next season whenever his carnival was close to the new troupe.

Financed by the understandably grateful Ijssel Taige, the three-person Corberrin Troupe enjoyed a week's rest in Sleespoken's major hotel, were booked into the Scoor Theatre, and fared very well indeed. Sleespoken was the natural place for them to begin their new lives. The Taige affair was a *cause célèbre*, and Rinegar a celebrity, throughout the city and the surrounding countryside. And, as word slowly spread—the telegraph was eighty years old on Bor— throughout the continent.

Corisande enjoyed numerous dates and spending sprees and loaded her hotel room with new clothing. Berneson, too, celebrated new wealth and popularity by buying clothes and by being magnanimously receptive to as many of his female fans as possible.

Rinegar conversed and asked questions, and spent much time in the library.

"There has never been a predator of major size on this planet," he said, shaking his head. The three were gathered in Berneson's hotel suite; he enjoyed living even more highly than he could afford.

"Never?"

"Well, never since humans came along, millions upon millions of years ago. Consequently, there have been many generalized animal-kills, because even worgs and cloars threatened to become far too numerous. That's the answer to what we call the 'backwardness' of these people. They developed far more slowly than man did on Earth—than the Azuli on Azul, too, you may be sure of that! Bor was old when Borean man came along, and far more geologically settled as a planet than earth was when our ancestors were spreading out from the Mediterranean and the Nile. So Boreans had fewer natural disasters to fight and endure. Nor did they have to be hunters. Herbivorous animals were so plentiful that they represented the only menace to Borean man's progress."

"Progress!" Berneson snorted, directing a meaningful glance at the primitive newspaper lying on the Borean equivalent of a coffee table.

"But—how did man ever develop in the first place?" Cory wanted to know.

Rinegar shrugged. "Who can say? Not Borean archaeologists and anthropologists. It's never occurred to them to ask the question. Borean man did, and he had it very easy indeed. As a consequence he never became a hunter. He slew some nearby meat animals, also taking their milk and learning to eat this and that flora. He was able to settle in one place, and he became an agriculturist very quickly. Oh, I tell you—in *agriculture* these people are far ahead of Earth when it was in the Model-T stage. Not in mechanization, of course. But knowledge of fertilizers and soil and crops, the ability to wrest every last morsel of food out of even tiny plots of earth—I mean bor. And naturally they see man and nature and animals in harmony; they are instinctive ecologists."

Berneson consulted his watch. "Got to go," he said, and he rose and departed. Another fan, doubtless.

"Jake, there are an awful lot of things we could do for these people," Cory said thoughtfully.

He studied her speculatively. "Cory, why? These people don't need doing for. They're happier than humans have ever been anywhere, I swear they are. Should we try to help them develop their automobiles, so that they can move faster and fill their sky with deadly fumes? Should we try to shove them toward air travel, so they can move even faster and pollute even more?"

She shook her head, frowning. "No, I see your point. But—what about medicine?"

"Right." He nodded, beaming. "What do you know about medicine, Cory?"

She sighed. "I see. Nothing. You?"

"Nothing. I've always licked my own cuts, which has made more than one medic throw up his hands. For anything more serious than that, I've gone to the medics, and they've either medicked me or put me into a Doctor for a while."

"A *Doctor!*" Cory cried, with a little shiver. "You've been in one of those iron wombs?"

"Yep. Listen, there used to be human doctors! Those old-time physicians treated everything—even operated. And they had headaches, bad nights, got angry . . . and just plain made mistakes, sometimes. Now we have the Doctors: macro-programmed supercomputers, combined with a wide range of abilities to take samples, run practically instant tests, and so on. They don't make mistakes. Human medics still treat the little things, and are otherwise technicians for the Doctors. The cybernetic devices we call Doctors both diagnose and prescribe—"

"And sometimes *treat,*" Cory said, nodding impatiently. She saw that Rinegar was about to continue his textbook description of the medical machines, and she just wasn't interested. She returned to the subject at hand: Bor: "Berneson . . . ," she began thoughtfully, but she shook her head. "No, he doesn't know anything about medicine, either. Wait a minute though, we *do* know some things. Antiseptic conditions . . ."

"The Boreans know too, Cory. They learned about sepsis and antisepsis and the medical value of sterilization, as close as they can get to it. Natural outgrowth of their tremendous knowledge of biology and damned decent knowledge of chemistry. They're *good* farmers, Core."

"Um. Well, uh—oh! What about vaccination? I mean, the concept of injecting someone with a *little* sickness so that he becomes immune to the big one—that is how it works, isn't it?"

Rinegar laughed, poking a finger at her nose. It was a dry, not-quite laugh, but it was close—a lot closer than those rare but frightening little almost-smiles he had used to vouchsafe, ghosts of smiles in which his eyes had not participated. He was changed, as they all three had changed.

"Yes, that's how it works, and they've got into that. About fifty years ago, there was a terrible epidemic: worg fever. The worgs died in droves. Milk and beef became scarce and prices rose. Some people bootlegged milk—can you imagine?—and those who drank it often became very sick, and many of them died. Local bioscientists worked hard, and finally one—a team, most likely, but one man's name is all there was in the book I read—finally one discovered a worg calf that had contracted the disease when it was three days old. They had separated it from its mother after the first day; she died. The calf became ill, but recovered."

"A little dose of mama's infected milk?"

He nodded. "That was the conclusion they got

around to eventually. So they invented inoculation, crudely. The worgs didn't take to being fed infected milk! They seemed to know instinctively that they shouldn't drink it. But those who did sickened—and lived." He shook his head and sighed. "It was another ten years before they tried the same process with human beings. The pro-inoculation physicians were called charlatans by their association, of course. But inoculation worked—of course."

"Ten years? It mightn't have taken less time than that on Earth, Jake!"

He nodded, sobering and gazing at the carpet between his feet. "Yes. But remember what I said: biology is advanced beyond technology here, and chemistry's coming right along. In physics they're—children." He sighed, raising his eyes again to her large blue ones.

"Think about it, Cory. Medicine came along slowly on Earth. We've always been *thing*-makers, and we've always spent a great deal more time and money figuring ways to kill animals and people than to keep them alive, and keep ecology balanced."

She nodded. They sat in reflective silence for a time, until one of them suggested they'd better vacate Berneson's suite. He did a lot of entertaining.

By the following summer, the Corberrin Troupe was accustomed to hotels and long train rides; to adulation and money and new clothing. Ringear was forced to enter a diet-and-exercise regimen: good eating and comfortable living had begun to show up in his belly and jowls. By the following summer, Berneson had to be got out of a bit of trouble involving an angry husband and a handsome wife. By the following summer, Corisande had fallen in love and toppled out again.

Berneson was frequently gone, and his companions knew from the newspapers and common talk that he was still enjoying himself, playing his little tricks and womanizing.

He also turned up very intoxicated indeed, with the latest model automobile—a Mark II.5—and with every evidence of having been left a fortune by a rich uncle.

Next morning there was the newspaper article about the bank robbery. Money had been taken from the locked vault of the Farmers' and Merchants' Bank of Chescore. Totally inexplicably, the vault was neither unlocked nor tampered with. No one in Chescore connected the mystery with the presence in their city of the Corberrin Troupe. No one but Corisande and Rinegar, and Berneson would admit absolutely nothing.

There was a scene, a loud and eventually violent one, and by evening Berneson was gone. Rinegar and Corisande searched and hired searchers, but they did not find him.

They took the train to the next city without him, and played there for two weeks without the -ber- of Cor-ber-rin.

"Do you think he'll ever come back, Jake?"

"I don't know," he admitted. "But I think I know this: if he does, we'd better just say nothing and hope he's, uh, gone straight."

Then came the news of the landing of a spaceship nine miles outside Sleespoken.

10

The Earthsider's composure fell from them like leaves from a tree in autumn.

They did not have to ask what the newcomers, the sky people, looked like when they emerged from their enormous craft nine miles outside Sleespoken.

They were short, the aliens, not uniform in height but shorter than Earthsiders or Boreans. They were very pale, almost white. Not white like bond paper; white like the stuff newspapers were printed on, on Bor, where paperback books had not yet been invented. Their complexion was uniform, and so was their hair. It was soft, silky-looking, and cloud-white. White, not blond like that of Corisande the Incredible.

The alien's eyes were as lacking in pigment as their flesh and their hair. And Corisande and Rinegar knew who and what the newcomers to Bor were, and whence they came.

They came from Azul. They were the Azuli.

They had been Earth Union's rival for a half-century, once contact was made as each race expanded its spatial frontiers. And they had been Earth's deadly enemy in a war that had now lasted nearly nineteen years.

"Oh, Jake! What shall we *do?*"

He shook his head, thinking. "Continue being Boreans," he said after a time. "Business as usual . . . during . . . alterations." He got the word out between twisted lips. "Earth has landed on a lot of peopled planets, and so has Azul. So—for Bor, it's the Azuli. But we do nothing, Cory, nothing. Not one untoward action or word. We continue. As Corberrin—or as Corrin without Berneson."

"And what if—what if—"

"Let's worry about the what-ifs when they come along, Core. They may see what a backward and quiet little planet this is and liftoff tomorrow."

But she had trouble getting to sleep, and she knew he had, too, despite his seeming calm and logical replies to her frightened questions. When she awoke in the morning, having had very bad dreams indeed, she was sure that he had. But she had resolved to say nothing more about it, and she didn't.

The Azuli did not liftoff tomorrow, or the tomorrow after that or the one after that. They had been on Bor five days when Berneson came—home.

Part 3

The Azuli

11

Cory suffered most, that was obvious. In just under a year on Bor she had changed the most. She had had sixteen years to practice being a spoiled, arrogant, and willfully undependable brat who was shipped up to the war zone because her talent was desperately needed—and who was shipped home because they were not *that* desperate.

But she was still a girl, far from through forming her life's personality and views and style.

Berneson, on the other hand, had now had over twenty-five years of practice at becoming Berneson and staying Berneson. Just as spoiled, just as contumacious, considerably less dependable, and afflicted with a seemingly innate wish to be Peck's Bad Boy. Neither of his companions could see that he had taken anything seriously yet, nor did he seem about to. Aside from the apprehension he shared with the others, of course: that the Azuli would find them and learn their origin and then their Powers, or guess at the latter and conclude the former and—do whatever they did to Earthsider spies. Only Rinegar knew.

Rinegar. He'd had fifty years, but somehow and somewhere he had either gotten over the natural arrogance of the spoiled psi's, or he had never been alllowed to develop it. Stern parents, perhaps. And he had found love, too, the real and true love that lasted beyond a lifetime. He alone of the trio had been a willing volunteer in the war with Azul. He alone had hurled himself into his work: spying, espionage, as a team with his beloved wife. He alone had seen action and known deadly peril many times; he alone of the three had been wounded.

And he had experienced what no man, no human being should ever have to experience. He had lived and shared, in his psionically facile mind, the death by torture of his wife. And he had, understandably, drawn well into himself, beginning the ancient process known as going to pieces. Because of his record and his experience, he had been commended, medalled, and sent home with honor.

And with his dreams, his ghastly memories, his bitterness. He had not wanted to return to Earth. He had wanted to be sent out again and again until perhaps, if he was fortunate enough, he would die swiftly. Perhaps some psychologist or other had made a careful notation that Rinegar might cherish a secret wish to die as his wife had, as expiation, perhaps, for volunteering and thus bringing her into the war and her death.

He avoided personal ties, edged and even strode away from close relationships, avoided and ignored and, on several occasions, insulted women. He had shown little concern in the matter of Berneson's having robbed the bank in Chescore; only Cory's reaction and her haranguing of Berneson and his blasting her with words, and threatening her as well, had drawn Rinegar into that.

Rinegar, he told Corisande, had cared: about his wife and about Earth and the war. Both wife and participation in the war had been taken from him. He would not allow himself to care again; he would not be crushed again.

"Ignore Berneson; let him destroy himself. And ignore the Azuli. So they are here. They are not our concern. We are rejects, remember. Earth doesn't want us. On this planet, we're forced to make a living traveling all about on these chuffing rattling things that pass as transportation: their abominable railroads and their ridiculously primitive trains."

It was far more bitter-sounding than he had been for a long, long time. Corisande turned her head a little to one side. *He doesn't want to care,* she thought. *And if he does care, he doesn't want to admit it or show it!* And she smiled within herself.

"Methinks the gentleman doth protest too much," she said, with a little smile.

Her smile crumpled when he stared at her a moment, his eyes altogether expressionless, and then rose and walked out of the room.

That was in the first month of summer, in the city called Ecore.

They saw the newspaper headlines together, in the city named Larl, in the second month of summer, which was also named Larl.

AZULI TO STAY, BUILD BASE ON BOR—TAKHNU

Takhnu was commander of the Azuli spaceship *Yorsh.*

"Stay," Berneson breathed, and in a glance Cory saw that the headline had made a serious breach in his mask of arrogant unconcern.

"A base," Rinegar muttered, and Cory looked at

him, too, and was astonished. His eyes! They were sharp, thoughtful, seeming to glitter in his face (jowly despite his exercises and dietary care).

It's taken the Azuli, she mused, *to put expression in his eyes!*

But they were dead embers again, the fire gone, a few moments later. They were eating their dinner in a small Larli restaurant where they hoped not to be recognized.

"So they're setting up a base right there near Sleespoken," he said quietly, picking up a menu. "So we no longer accept engagements in Sleespoken."

"But that's where we're more popular than anywhere else!" Berneson exclaimed, sitting forward.

Rinegar only stared at him.

After a while Berneson jerked his head down in a sharp nod and bent over his menu. "You're right," he muttered.

But after that they often wore a common expression of apprehension. And they noticed a sudden decrease in stories about the Azuli. Borean lack of curiosity—or Azuli orders?

By the third month of summer they had gained a bit of a reputation for temperament, after their refusal to accept a very attractive engagement in Sleesponken. They had also learned the news that more and more people knew and whispered about—and that the newspapers did not mention, ever.

The Azuli were not only building a base on Bor, they were—operating. There had been a simple and brief and awe-inspiring demonstration of their weaponry. There had been mandates. They had constructed a great fence from some pre-cut material from their ship, and within it they were constructing their buildings. Already they had herded within an even one hundred Borean males, all between sixteen and twenty-two. The boys had not come out.

"Conscript labor," Berneson murmured. "Agh, the sparmy flainers!" It had been nearly a year since they'd heard a piece of the copious slang of Mars from his lips.

"They're forcing young Boreans to do their manual labor for them?"

"Of course."

"Or . . . worse," Rinegar said thoughtfully. "The ship left, and the one that came back was a different craft. That would tend to indicate a long trip; the second ship must have left Azul—or wherever it was based—at the same time the first one left here. Maybe earlier. They know what they're doing, and they knew in advance. That second spacer brought more construction materials, of course."

"And some more machinery for communications, and weaponry and . . . detection gear?" Berneson licked his lips, frowning meditatively.

Rinegar sat back. "Suppose—suppose they sent one hundred Boreans . . . elsewhere. A payload both ways: the returning ship brought whatever they needed here. As you said."

"Oh no!" Cory said, sitting forward and slapping her hands onto the table so that the silver jumped and jingled. "No, no! Not to send them out against— against the Earth Union!"

"We don't know that," Berneson pointed out.

"No, we don't and we won't until we hear that they've taken in another batch of conscripts."

They heard that two weeks later.

Corisande: That's *awful!* We've got to do something!"

Rinegar: "It is none of our concern."

Berneson: "I'm all through worrying about this sort of stuff. We're out of the war, outcasts. So the Azuli grab a few of these local yokels. So?"

The newspaper: "General Takhnu has advised Premier Feevoke that the Azuli will be most happy to introduce machinery to Borean farmers, that they might increase productive capacity and thus not be forced to exercise such care in limiting the size of their families."

The little man in Sprencore: "Them Azuli! Steen knows what they're building in there, or where they're putting all those people. A week ago they took my nephew Rej, and another boy off the farm just over the hill. Said they'd pay'em well, teach'em a lot, too. But they weren't *asking* Rej and his father. They were *telling*."

The newspaper: AZULI SKYSHIP
                  DEPARTS AGAIN

The newspaper: CORBERRIN DRAWS
                  RECORD AUDIENCE
                  IN SMEENCORE

Corisande: "They *are!* They're forcing those boys to go and help them fight—against Earth!"

Berneson: "So what? They're just primitives, farmers. So what?"

Rinegar: "It isn't any of our business. We're rejects, outcasts. Earth High Command doesn't want us. And what difference can a few Borean boys make in this war?"

The newspaper: AZULI SKYSHIP YORSH

RETURNS WITH LOAD
OF FRESH SUPPLIES

The newspaper: CORBERRIN TROUPE
                 OPENING TONIGHT
                 IN SPRENCORE'S
                 MEMORIAL CENTER

"You dance beautifully, Cory," Brool Erquen told the slim blonde he had been lucky enough to pry away from the Memorial Center after her performance with her uncle and blood-cousin.

"It's easy with you, Brooly." She smiled. "But the music just stopped."

Laughing, he took her back to their table. The other two couples were there before them, their heads close together as they all bent forward across the candle-lit table. They jerked apart as Brool and his famous date returned to the table.

"Hey, what's the deep conversation?" Cory asked smiling, and received such a concerted and unsmiling stare that she sobered in an instant.

After a silent moment, the girl named Evreh asked, "What do you think of the Azuli, cousin?"

Cory forced her face to remain open and impassive. "Hardly at all," she said lightly. "I had hoped our sun would do something for that ghastly pallor of theirs, though. They—"

"Do you know they're sending Borean boys somewhere . . . else? In their skyships?"

Corisande's mask slipped. She took care to restore it, looking both surprised and unbelieving. She narrowed her eyes, putting her head a bit on one side.

"What do you mean? Where?"

Evreh shook her head. "Somewhere. We don't

know. But they've *collected* five hundred, and there just isn't *room* for all of them in that iron camp of theirs. Think about it. The ships that leave and return; the boys they round up and take inside. No one's ever seen one of them again. And they want us to have more children!"

Cory looked around at them. They were all gazing fixedly at her, very serious young people, two Borean girls and three boys. All were within the Azuli conscription age. She wished Rinegar were here, wished she had Rinegar's Power, rather than this silly poltie-thing she couldn't even use. What were they thinking? Something striking about those faces: they did not look *scared*. They were deeply serious, concerned. Determined?

"You," she said, looking slowly from one intense face to the next, "you're—testing me!"

She chewed her lip thoughtfully, her eyes leaping from one red-brown Borean face to the next. The one girl wore her hair in traditional short bob; the other's was long, past her shoulders. One saw quite a bit of that, now, among the young: they were imitating the famous female member of the Corberrin troupe.

"Those boys need help," the short-haired girl said, she who'd spoken first. She was again bent forward over the table, her arms and hand on it as though poised, her eyes like black coals about to flash into bright flame.

Cory nodded slowly. "Yes," she said very quietly. "How, though? What's being done?"

"Evreh," her escort said, but she shook her head. "Corisande is all right. She's young. Aren't you all right, cousin Corisande?"

He's warning her, Cory thought. *I—I might be in danger! If they get the idea I'm NOT all right, that is.*

They're doing something—they're . . . my gosh! There's an underground, a resistance group!

She straightened up and drew a deep breath, let it out as she looked around the candle-lit room full of young Boreans dancing and engaging in whatever conversations they considered worthwhile. And here, at this table, sat five members of some sort of group—a protest group, perhaps, or . . . perhaps more. Serious, intense, dedicated-looking, and—*not scared.*

"Let's get out of here," Cory said.

Brool frowned. "Why?"

"I'll stay with Evreh tonight so that you can all be sure you can trust me. In the morning we'll go to the bank. Evreh will act as if she isn't with me. I'll cash a check. My money's in Sprencore, not here. I have an idea you five will find something to do with the cash, won't you?"

"She knows," Evreh's date exclaimed in a whisper.

Cory shook her head. "I know that the Azuli are taking people like you and Brool and Horje, too, into that iron fence of theirs, and that they aren't coming out. I know that all three of you are the right age, and I know that I'm female and Evreh and I don't have to like some—*creatures* taking our males. I *think* someone must be doing something about it. No one's ever tried to take action without having a desperate need for money. Well, I have money."

They left the restaurant.

Next day Cory cashed the large check, waiting while a wire was sent to her bank—with apologies, dear cousin Corisande, and I certainly enjoyed your performance last night—and was answered. She walked out of the bank with her Borean beltbag stuffed with money. She stood outside, looking up and down the street as though deciding which way to go, and a noisy Norbeek Mark II pulled over: a taxicab.

While Cory leaned in to talk briefly with the driver, Evreh emerged from the bank and climbed into the taxi. When it drove off, Cory's belt-purse was empty. She was Involved.

The Azuli ground truck hummed along, its superb shock-absorber system taking most of the roughness out of the ride on the reprehensible Borean road. With the Azuli rode one Borean; someone had to help them locate natives of the proper age, and collaborators have ever been plentiful among any race on any planet.

He directed them up the side road between a fenced field of cover crop, which was barely breaking the soil, and thirty or so worgs grazing directly across the road from it. They pulled up in front of the farmhouse. All five of them climbed out, short and very pale humanoids wearing pale green Azuli uniforms and squared caps. Four wore side arms. The fifth, who remained beside the truck's hood, carried a whistler. The Borean fingerman remained in the cab.

The four Azuli crossed the yard, glancing this way and that in the twilight. Two rounded the house; the others knocked on the front door. A woman answered, and went pale and wide-eyed. She did not scream, nor did her husband resist. Their older son was assisted up into the back of the truck, and two

Azuli climbed in after him, then a third. The driver took his place behind the stick. The one with the whistler carried easily in the crook of his arm climbed in on the other side, beside the collaborator.

They backed up and drove away. Behind them on the porch, the farmer stood with his arm around his sobbing wife, gazing after the vehicle's rolling dust cloud.

Back on the highway, the truck was forced to stop after about a mile. Some young idiots had got their wagon sidewise across the road and were having trouble getting it out. It was loaded with hay. The driver revved his engine and buttoned his siren briefly. The three young Boreans who were working about the wagon glanced up and resumed work. One of them waved a hand helplessly.

The Azuli had a choice. Wait, or help. Those idiots were draft-age. . . . The Boreans looked up as four Azuli came swaggering toward them. They turned back to their wagon and its load of hay—

—which was hurled back as two other young Boreans rose from beneath it. The first launched his pitchfork in a fluid motion. It seemed to waver strangely in flight and then drive into the whistler-man's throat. He went down without a sound, and already another pitchfork was taking the driver in the throat, and the other two Azuli went down before they had their side arms out of their holsters. Each wore a pitchfork in the throat. There had been hardly a sound, but there had been a little, and one of the Borean teeners was loping forward even as his three-pronged spear took its target with uncanny precision, in the throat.

The boy, on one knee, picked up the whistler. Two of his companions moved swiftly toward the truck, pitchforks poised like javelins. And the fifth Azuli came out of the truck and hurrying around it, drawing his pistol.

Both boys launched their three-tined spears and fell flat. The Azuli pistol sent its charge slashing over their heads as its wielder gurgled. The spear launched an instant before the other drove into his throat. The other, heading rather wide of its mark, suddenly swerved and plunged into his falling body.

"How does this thing work?" the boy with the whistle gun cried in frustration, and the sixth member of the group rose from beneath the hay and hurried to show him.

"Can you do it?"

"I can do it. He was leading them to us. I can do it."

And he did, using the Azuli weapon on the Azuli collaborator as he climbed out of the Azuli truck.

Within five minutes the wagonload of hay was trundling away across the field. Left behind was the Azuli truck, bearing a runny sign just painted on it, in Borean, and one Borean traitor and five Azuli—without weapons.

"So they're becoming civilized," Rinegar said behind his morning paper. "They're learning to kill." He shook his head and sighed. "The Sons of Freedom indeed—that's been used so many times it's a cliché everywhere else but here. Wait a minute—this is impossible! All five of the Azuli were killed with pitchforks *directly through the throats.*" He raised his eyes to stare across the table at Berneson.

"Where was this?"

"Less than ten miles from here," Rinegar answered, then his eyes left the other man to look past him. Berneson half turned as Corisande joined them. She sat down with a quiet "good morning," followed by a yawn.

"Why so yawny this morning, Core?" Berneson asked. "You're not getting to be an old woman, are you?"

"She was . . . out last night," Rinegar said in an abstracted voice, staring at her with one eyebrow raised.

"Oh? A little of the nightlife, eh?" Berneson said, still grinning. "Where were you, Incred—" He broke off, his mouth remaining open. His eyes were wide as he looked from her to Rinegar, glanced at the paper, looked back at her again.

"I'd say she was about—ten miles out of town," Rinegar said, in that same not-quite-present, not-quite-believing voice.

"On a hayride," Berneson muttered, but the girl was not looking at either of them.

She said nothing. Rinegar gnawed his lip, staring.

After a while Berneson said, "I'll bet it was fun!"

13

On the afternoon of the day after losing five of their press-gangers, the Azuli made their first arrest on Bor. The culprit was the assiduous newspaper editor who had run the story. The city seemed to swarm with green uniforms and white faces, and there were Azuli skimmers overhead and Azuli cars on the roads. None attended the performance of Corberrin, however. The aliens were entirely too busy to go and watch a trio of the local entertainers of this primitive planet.

An Azuli groundcar was holed and wrecked as it drove along the road not five miles from town; the Borean teener with the Azuli pistol was slain easily and brought into town. The story had been printed, and apparently the invaders felt they might as well let all know that retribution could be swift and ugly. Cory summed it up: "Bor is shuddering."

Three days later someone, somewhere, printed up a batch of leaflets and strewed them all over town and out into the country, tucked into mailers from a hardware store holding its annual pre-winter sale. They related a new tale of the underground.

This story was even more incredible, given a little thought. Ten young men had been in the back of a Azuli conscript truck. The Azuli guard, armed with one of their two-handed sonic guns called whistlers, had stood at his post while his four fellows went thirstily across the street to sample some local refreshment. He had not moved from his post at the tail end of the truck. The steel tailgate, only entry into the truck's steel van, had been locked. The time was ten in the morning.

Naturally he paid little attention to the noises within, to the occasional creaking of the truck with the movement of the ten primitives he and his companions had recruited the evening before.

Eventually his fellows returned, bringing him a couple of bottles, and asking if everything was all right. Not until then, so the story went, did he realize that the vehicle was strangely silent. He mentioned it. His chief unlocked and opened the truck.

It was empty.

"No Sons of Liberty sign this time, I notice," Rinegar said, putting down the pamphlet. "*If* this is true."

"It's true," Cory said. She smiled at Berneson. "Isn't it, Bernie?"

"I forgot the sign," he said.

"Bernie," she said, still smiling at him, "was *out* last night. I'll bet it was fun!"

They finished their breakfast in silence. Cory and Bernie exchanged secret smiles and rolled their eyes at each other from time to time, pretending Ringar wasn't there. But they said nothing.

Stirrring his after-breakfast cup of drim, Ringar leaned back. He glanced around, then spoke.

"All right. We agreed not to get involved. But you, Cory, aided and abetted a resistance group by mind-directing the pitchforks they threw at the Azuli press-gang. And you, Bernie: you teleported into that truck, and out, and back inside, didn't you? Ten times. You must be a little tired and sore this morning, carrying those conscripts to wherever you teeported them. Right?"

Berneson yawned and flexed his arms elaborately. "Fortunately they aren't taking fat ones. It was fun, Jake." He reached over to slap the pamphlet. "Reading about it's fun, too." He leaned back, smiling.

Cory leaned forward intensely. "These people need *help*," she said, in a low voice as full of resolve as her face. "This is awful, what they're doing to Bor! *We* could do something about it." She shot Berneson a glance. "And not because it's 'fun.' All right, I've *been* helping. I've given them money. Then when I learned what they planned to try the other night, I knew they'd never succeed—not against guns. But if they couldn't miss with whatever missiles they threw—So I went along. I lay there in the hay, staring, and yes, I directed every one of those pitchforks to the target. If I'd known there was a fifth Azuli in the back of the truck, I'd have sent one around after him, too! And if you'd been with me, Jake, you'd have *known* he was there. He might have killed one of those boys."

Ringar sat silent, waiting for her to wind down. When she did, her nostrils flaring and her eyes very bright, he smiled at her.

"Corberrin has some mail this morning," he said, laying the document on the table. "That"—tapping it as the others fixed their gazes on the definitely non-Borean paper—"is an invitation. Command performance, I believe, is the proper phrase. We're to present a private performance for none less than General Takhnu."

"The chief of the monsters," Corisande whispered, picking up the folded paper. "Oh, yes! What a wonderful chance!"

"Now wait a minute," Berneson said, frowning and reaching for the invitation from the planetary "governor" from Azul. "That is about the most dangerous situation I can think of!"

Rinegar nodded. "I'll tell you what, Bernie," he said, "I'll tell you what. You think of a way to tell His Generalship and boss-ship that we are very sorry but we won't be able to put on a show for his noble self and staff, and we'll discuss it. Otherwise we'd better discuss other things."

Cory cocked an eyebrow. "Other things?"

"Yes. Bernie says that's dangerous: it is. He also said wait a minute, as though there were any question of our declining this invitation: there isn't. That does not decrease the danger, though. We're going to have to plan carefully, and *be* mighty careful, the whole time we're there."

"We have a week to prepare," Cory said.

"Yes, and notice that he must've checked our present engagement: he's invited us for the third day after we finish here."

"Sparm," Berneson muttered. "I was looking forward to a week off!"

Somehow Corisande could not help laughing.

A week later they checked into the hotel in Slee-spoken, and late that afternoon a handsome and stream-

lined Azuli groundcar came to convey them to alien
headquarters on Bor. Neither Bor nor Azuli knew
that it was aliens meeting aliens.

14

The multi-building complex forming General
Takhnu's domain was a slice of Azul on Bor. The
three Earthsiders didn't have to pretend surprise at
the gleaming technologia, but they were careful to si-
mulate awe and complete lack of comprehension. Corisande had been walking through autodoors all her
life, up until the past year on Bor. Now she gasped
and shrank back a little when the big metal door
wheeped open at her approach.

Their Azuli escort chuckled.

They walked into a wall-lit hallway and along it to
a steel stairway behind a door from the corridor; apparently Bor was not so important and Takhnu not so
influential as to have grav-plates here in his complex
of two-story buildings. They ascended green-painted
steel steps framed within blue-painted walls. Ahead of
them went a green-clad and emphatically white humanoid with white hair beneath his squared Azuli
cap. He was short, as they were all short. Behind them
came another, still explaining to Rinegar how the door
worked.

The building complex formed an almost perfect
square. Headquarters and officers' quarters, this building. Then there were barracks and armory and tool-
house and controls and power source and garages and
storage and—that other building. Another barracks.

Windowless. A prison, then—housing for the Borean conscripts. Approximately half the space within the square formed a courtyard for those press-ganged boys, that they could have sunlight and exercise while they waited. While they waited to be loaded into the great ship whose gleaming bulk reared skyward just outside the base, near a tall tower like an old-fashioned oil well.

Corisande saw some of the boys through a corridor window as they went upstairs. She said nothing, only biting her lip.

General Takhnu, like many other generals whether Earthsider or Azuli, was a big man who had been powerfully muscled and who was now going soft and jowly. His chest surged, but now his belly surged even farther, resting on his broad belt and circular buckle. He was losing his hair, too, and the fringe that remained was the pure white of summer clouds.

He beamed at them, with a great show of comity.

"Se renowned Corberrins! You are very welcome here, my friends, and I hope our food is to your liking. Corisande, I believe: you are more beautiful than your posters, my dear, and it is hard to believe that one so attractive and young could be so talented! And you are Berneson."

Berneson nodded, squaring his shoulders and giving the Azuli general a ceremonious nod of the head rather than a bow. The alien did not offer to shake hands or grip forearms, fortunately. Berneson was uncomfortable enough, just being here within the lair of the enemy. One slip—one intuitive Azuli guess—and not only their careers but their freedom and very possibly their lives were forfeit.

"Ah, and Rinegar, the mentalist. Will you tell me,

cousin," Takhnu said, adopting the local form of address, "if it is all brilliant illusion and planning, or do you in truth ["troos"] possess some extraordinary mental ability? Can you really read minds sir?"

There was but one answer Rinegar could give, that of the constant showman. In all the centuries of their existence, when had any of the charlatans calling themselves mentalists ever admitted to using tricks and research and secret assistants?

"Why, of course I read minds, General," he said. "Is there no such ability among the Azuli?"

There was not, he knew. Not aside from charlatanry. The Azuli had not, so far as anyone knew, developed psi-Powers. There was no explanation for the lack, any more than there was an explantion for the fact that Earthsiders, the race of genus *Homo terris,* had. Genus almost-*Homo azulis* just . . . hadn't.

Takhnu returned a dry little Azuli chuckle, the rustling of fallen leaves in an autumnal breeze. His collar was high and gold-braided and uncomfortable-looking, and there were gilded epaulets on his broad shoulders and at the cuffs of his uniform jacket.

"Sen perhaps you will read my mind and tell me what we are going to have for dinner, Cousin Rinegar?"

Rinegar laughed right back. "Ah, General, one does not flaunt one's abilities so."

"And Corberrin performs its miracles only for audiences, and for money, eh?"

"Exactly, General, exactly." Rinegar's dark eyes met the pale, almost unpigmented ones of the Azule for a moment, straight on. And caught the thought swiftly, easily from Takhnu's mind:

A cocky charlatan! Sese people wis all seir travels

and contacts could be of some value to us. . . .

They were introduced to several aides, including a colonel with Military Intelligence written all over his bearing and eyes and manner, so obviously that he might as well have worn a big red M.I. on his high forehead. Another could not take his eyes off Corisande, who was a good two inches taller than he.

The renowned Corberrins then had to mask another reaction, as food and drink were brought from another room—by Borean girls, all of whom appeared to be somewhere around Corisande's age. All wore short, sleeveless, square-necked Azuli tunics of various pastel shades, green and blue and yellow and lavender. They said nothing, absolutely nothing, and they kept their eyes down.

Slaves, Corisande thought, even as a smiling Takhnu explained how he was pleased to provide employment for native citizens.

"I should like to check the stage and the equipment, and the acoustics," Rinegar said, walking past the flower-bedecked table toward the stage. It was at the far end of the room, obviously constructed and equipped especially for Corberrin.

"The food—" Takhnu began, but subsided. Playing the role of the artiste with ease, for he had grown accustomed to it, Rinegar was striding on, followed by Corisande and Berneson.

They wandered about on the platform, floored with a chlorotic Azuli plastic, and Rinegar highhandedly directed Colonel Farshu to stand back against the far wall. With a glance at his general, Farshu obeyed. Rinegar then asked him again and again, in varying tones, whether he could be heard at that distance. To his companions Rinegar muttered, "Do *not* ask why they're all wearing nasal plugs."

They joined the noseplugged Azuli for dinner, then, and it was no less difficult than they had expected. Azuli questions were penetrating and were repeated or rephrased if the answers were not of sufficient depth; Corberrin questions were fielded or half-answered or, in some cases, ignored.

"Regrettably we haven't the facilities for a suitable demonstration of your amazing talents, Corisande," Takhnu said, "but we erected a few pitiful targets and provided bose targets and balls sat you might astonish my staff wis some few of your feats."

She smiled. "I admit to being nervous, General, and I admit also that I have been known to miss."

As they moved to the stage, the three Earthsiders glanced out a window into the courtyard—in time to witness the arrival of several trucks. All disgorged male Borean teen-agers. The trio exchanged looks, but proceeded with their performance.

They were all three careful to miss, now and again. After one of his deliberate failures, Berneson stepped into the booth and leaned back to grin at his uniformed audience.

"The trouble with command performances," he said, "is that this booth is of your construction, not mine!"

The Azuli laughed, nodding; even the Intelligence colonel. The remark had been designed to make them think there was indeed some trickery in Berneson's impossible act, and it was effective.

But Berneson's nervousness increased when Colonel Skarsh—the Intelligence man—insisted on volunteering. Making trebly certain that the booth's curtain was securely closed behind him, Bernie teeported into the wings to grin at Rinegar. There was no little concealed hole here for him to peer through. He had to content himself with a three-way relay: Corisande stood smiling at the volunteer, concentrating on broadcasting what she saw. Just behind her but out of sight behind the stage curtains, Ringar picked up her thoughts and whispered them to Berneson, who teeported back into the booth.

He stepped out behind Colonel Skarsh. "The officer from Azul," he proclaimed, "has his fingers laced together, backward, with one thumb thrust into his tunic. The right thumb, of course."

Skarsh turned with a look of amaze. "How do you know sis?"

Berneson smiles. "A performer does not reveal the secrets of his trade," he said, "any more than an officer reveals his strategy. But I can tell you this much: your elbows were at rest, so that I knew your activity was static, and as to which thumb—you'd have had to contort to get your left thumb into your tunic, Colonel." Berneson bowed, having given the impression he was a clever observer and little more.

The others laughed and applauded. But Skarsh was frowning as he returned to his seat, and he seemed to watch even more closely. Berneson deliberately made a half-miss next time.

Ringar, supremely confident in possessing a Power none could discover, performed as always. He included the usual miss and dramatic hesitations as he named the card or object the audience participant held up, concealed from him but visible to the rest of the onlookers. He chose to miss at identifying the mini-communicator in Major Yorshu's gloved hand, then admitted blandly that it was most difficult for a man of even his great powers to identify properly something he had never seen or heard of. And Yorshu apologized!

The young women Takhnu was so kind as to employ here in his steel-and-plastic fortress, as cooks and servants and perhaps more, were generously allowed to watch the performance. They were enthusiastic, although now and again one, looking nervous at her delighted outburst of applause, would glance in embarrassment at the Azuli. Delighted at the break in their presumably dull evenings on this alien and primitive planet, the Azuli paid them no attention. They were too busy laughing and applauding and bobbing their heads, beaming at the performers and at one another.

Corisande should not have done it, but she had exercised all the restraint she was capable of. She topped off the performance by holding high the glove Skarsh had "accidentally" left behind. She assumed it contained a microminiaturized recorder with which the Azuli intelligencer hoped to pick up some of the performers' conversation—hopefully incriminating or at least useful.

"The good colonel enjoyed the performance so much," she cried, smiling with ingenuous brightness, "that he forgot his gauntlet! I now return it to him!" And she aimed and threw the glove—and mind-guided it into the plate before him. It contained his half-finished dessert, and the glove landed with enough force to splash some raspberry-colored fruit and whipped cream onto his immaculate tunic.

Cory of course apologized. Skarsh's compatriots and commander laughed uproariously. Skarsh resembled a volcano about to blow its top.

It was Berneson who glanced out the window as they left the stage. "Jake," he said, and Rinegar glanced his way, tightened his mouth, and said nothing. "Ah," Berneson said, smiling he walked toward the audience, "I see some more of my countrymen for whom employment is being provided. And when are these being sent off in the great skyship?"

"Wha—what?"

Berneson beamed at Takhnu, surrounded by officers with faces similar to his: all flabbergasted and concerned.

"Ah, General, we of Bor know that you're secretly sending our brightest youths elsewhere. We think it's wonderful—you are educating them to return and help Bor reach the greatness and wisdom of your own world, aren't you?"

"I had not realized we were so . . . transparent," Takhnu said, glancing at Skarsh, who was still dabbing at his uniform with his napkin. He shot a steely look at Berneson, who grinned.

"Oh yes," Berneson said. "And when are they leaving? Will we be able to see the rising of the skyship? *That* is a performance I'd rather see than Corberrin, any day!"

"Ah . . . not for . . . a while, I'm afraid," Takhnu said, looking no less uncomfortable. "You will of course accept our hospitality for se night, but my car will return to your hotel tomorrow. I am afraid you will miss se ship's departure."

"Will they bring us knowledge of your people's marvelous transportation and weaponry?"

"In . . . time," Takhnu said. "You understand sat learning of such sings is not se matter of a week, or even a year. But—"

Berneson had to get his questions asked, and surely a successful performer could interrupt even a general. "Might we see some of the things we know of, the strange weapons that I have heard operate somehow by sound? Do you keep them here?" He glanced around, as though expecting to find a whistler propped against the wall of the great parlor.

Takhnu's smile was tight. "I am sure sat a man in your line of work can hardly be interested in such, Cousin Berneson."

Bernie sighed elaborately, but maintained his smile. "Ah, I see. I would not tell you my secrets and you wil not share yours with me!"

Takhnu chuckled. "Exactly," he said nodding, obviously delighted to have his "explanation" provided for him. "We are bose, after all, professionals, isn't it?"

Little flainer doesn't speak Borean any better than they do Earthish, Berneson thought. But he had more questions, and they had to be asked, and now. "All this space, and all constructed so *rapidly!*" he said, again looking about as though marveling at Azuli genius. "One would think—how many of your people are on our world, General?"

Naturally Takhnu didn't answer that one either, or the next: were they all here, within the confines of the base?

Berneson passed a hand across his brow, rather overdramatically. "I can't speak for the Azuli general and his staff, but the combination of fine food and a difficult performance weary me more than a day's work on a farm!" He shook his head. "I believe that I shall be able to sleep," he said, smiling at Skarsh, "even though I shall feel a little nervous, under the marvels of your mechanical surveillance."

Affecting to look shocked rather than insulted, Takhnu assured the performers that they would be under no such surveillance. He thanked them again, brought his aides to their feet with him in offering a toast, and expressed his sincere wish that Corberrin would be nothing but comfortable. Major Yorshu would show them to their suite.

A suite it was, on the other side of the hall, meaning they could not look out upon the conscripts' courtyard below. Berneson and Rinegar had separate rooms opening onto a parlor. Beyond that was the bathroom, with Cory's room adjoining it. With a last enthusiastic babble about their performance and how pleased and happy and grateful he was, fat Major Yorshu departed, closing the door.

Crossing immediately to it, Berneson pulled it open. "It isn't locked," he muttered in surprise, then called a last goodnight to Yorshu, who had turned frowning. Berneson closed the door and locked it. Then he walked to the bathroom. "How nice that they have water here, rather than sonicleansers!" And he wrenched on both sink and both shower taps. "There!" He smiled at his companions, beckoning. Cory and Jake walked over to him, standing just outside the bathroom. The rushing water from the four faucets was loud in the room.

"I hope that doesn't lessen the water pressure for whatever poor creature has to wash out Skarsh's tunic," Bernie said, giving Cory a mock-admonitory look. "Naughty naughty!" And he looked at Rinegar. "Did you get it all, Jake?"

"Very clever of you, Bernie. Particularly that last—if this room is bugged, neither Takhnu nor Skarsh knows about it. But all that rushing water will certainly drown out our voices, if there are listening or recording devices in here." He turned a chastening gaze on the girl. "I can't say the same for you, Cory. Splashing dessert on his coat isn't exactly the best way to gain the favor of an Azuli Military Intelligencer!" But he smiled. "On the other hand—it was delightful." He squeezed her shoulder. "Now. Although I detected no thoughts of this room's being bugged from either Takhn's or Skarsh's minds when

Bernie cleverly gave them the lead, he's turned all this water on to cover our voices."

She glanced at Berneson, who gave her his mocking bow. But when his head came up, all trace of smile was gone. "I once read or heard," he said, staring at nothing and they had to lean forward to hear him, "that you can read about a hundred atrocities and hear about a thousand, with little effect. But you need *see* only one. And then a total stranger becomes your—brother." He closed his eyes. "Well, he isn't a total stranger, but I recognized one of the new conscripts." He opened his eyes to stare at her, then looked at Rinegar. "I called Jake aloud, thought *listen* as hard as I could, and tried to send what I saw. Then I started asking Takhnu all those questions."

Cory looked at Rinegar.

"Bernie saw Junty Grenn," he said.

Her hands rushed to her cheeks. "Oh *no!*"

Berneson nodded. "Oh yes. And that was it. At that moment, it all became clear and . . . *necessary.*"

"What—what do you mean, Bernie?" Tears sparkled in Cory's eyes, making them misty.

Berneson glanced from her to Rinegar.

"I mean no more funning around, no more ostrich stuff, burying my head in Borean sand. I have just declared war on Azul!"

"Oh, *Ber*-nie!" Cory said delightedly, practically jumping at him and hugging him.

"Here, stop that," he said, disentangling her. "Look, these Azuli endanger *me.* I've got a nice life here; never had it so nice. Skarsh acted suspicious, whether Jake saw it in his mind or not. We'll be watched hereafter, and checked, and one day—Well, I'm not going to wait. Earth can go blow itself up, for all I care. But I want the Azuli off *my* planet—off *Bor!*"

"Oh," Corisande said quietly, stepping back.

"I asked General Tacky a lot of questions I was sure he wouldn't answer, but the idea was he *would* answer, whether he knew it or not. Well, Jake, did he?"

Ringar nodded. "There are two hundred and sixty Azuli on this planet, counting ten sick, and as of tonight they are all here, in this complex. That's because of the answer to another of your questions: the shipload of conscripts leaves tomorrow."

"Tomorrow!"

"With Junty Grenn," Cory whispered.

Ringar nodded. "That's right. And it isn't all. Takhnu's sending an aide to Azul with an urgent request. He's in trouble from more than underground resistance here; he doesn't seem to think that's too important. But he's lost nineteen men in the past two months, from some sort of illness. Name and cause unknown. It pops up and kills Azuli, quickly. There are six on the ship out there now, isolated, with the ship's Doctor and sentient medics, too, trying to figure out what's wrong."

Berneson cocked an eyebrow. "Tough! Something peculiar to Bor, hm? But apparently it doesn't affect us."

"Maybe we've just been lucky," Cory said, "so far."

Berneson shook his head. "I doubt that. I'd say we're immune. Either the Boreans are too, or whatever it is just takes a mild form with them."

"Takhnu's medics *think* they've isolated it," Ringear said. "But they haven't found a way to treat it, much less immunize. That's what Takhnu wants from Azul: medics or an order to clear off Bor!"

Berneson narrowed his eyes. "If I thought they might adopt the latter course . . ."

"You wouldn't just let them ship Junty Grenn off to some Azuli labor camp or whatever they're doing with those boys!"

"They're sending the Boreans to an unpeopled planet of a system the other side of the Azuli system," Ringear said. "As slaves, yes, but not in fighting or experimentation. They're there to raise crops."

"The Azuli need more food, hmm?"

"That's still helping them in the war against Earth!" Cory cried, and her teeth sank into her lower lip. "Junty Grenn—a *slave!* A farmer under a strange sun, raising foodcrops to feed the Azuli who're killing Earthsiders!"

"Damn Earth!" Berneson snapped. "Understand: it isn't Earth I'm interested in, Cory. It's—wait a minute. Jake? How'd you know so much?"

Ringear smiled rather diffidently. "I thought of the idea before you did, Bernie. I was tapping their minds all I could, even while we ate. Over-Colonel Ketru's a medic, and I got a few little items from his mind. The point is that all of them are worried, because their men are scared. That's why Takhnu brought us here, to provide a little entertainment and relieve the minds of the general staff. I imagine we'll be asked back, to perform for the whole lot of them next. Now, my advice is to wait and plan, and by then we'll have had plenty of time to think of a way to—"

"Wait!" The color rushed to Cory's cheeks as she

interrupted angrily, "But—Junty!"

Rinegar sighed. "War," he said, quoting an ancient homily, "is hell."

Her chin rose. "Bor—and Junty—are not at war!"

Berneson shrugged. "Jabber jabber jabber. I told you what I intend to do. Are you two going to help me, or stand by while I handle a one-man war?"

"Bernie, you know I'm ready," the girl said. Suddenly she turned an apprehensive frown on Rinegar. "Jake—what about those girls, the servants? What are they doing with them?"

"I don't want to talk about that," he said, and she gasped. He sighed, looked down, and nodded. "It's either join you or kill you. Anything you do now will implicate me. When were you planning on acting on this declaration of war, Bernie?"

"Tonight."

"Tonight! We can't—"

Once again Berneson amazed them: "Please hush, Jake," he said firmly. "What about the answer to an implied question: where's the armory?"

"The triangular yellow building," Rinegar said, "but—"

Berneson sighed. "Oh man! This is going to be just lovely—well, I may as well risk it. I've been lucky ever since we plopped down on Bor. Maybe it'll hold tonight." He gave them a sardonic grin, the old wicked look they knew he cultivated. "In case the luck of Berneson ends right now, it's been sheer boredom knowing you two." And he grinned, and closed his eyes, and—vanished.

Berneson materialized in a huge dark room full of packing crates. He was about two meters inside the wall forming the base of the pyramid-shaped building, which he hoped would be the best place to teleport himself. He could not be one hundred percent sure of his directions and his brain's unusual sense of *place*, not when he was moving himself to where he'd never been. But he assumed there'd be crates stacked against the wall, and he couldn't be certain of their size. He was not anxious to appear either within a wall or a case full of Azuli weaponry!

At the last moment he changed his mind, mentally changing his destination from the armory floor to a point precisely one-half meter above it. Thus he was saved from rematerializing with his legs in a crate, but he dropped a few centimeters to the top of it with a painful jolt and a grunt. Losing his balance, he fell off onto a concrete floor. And was very still and silent, holding his breath while he listened for some indication that he'd been heard.

Apparently no one had heard. Armories were not apt to be occupied at night, and certainly weren't guarded *inside,* not on a planet where there were none of that enemy the Azuli hated above all others: teleporters. And he had not made enough noise, Berneson decided after a minute or so, to arouse the guard or guards that were certainly outside the building.

He rose, breathing a relieved sigh: his ankle wasn't sprained, although his elbow hurt a little. He looked around, waiting for his eyes to grow accustomed to the darkness. They did, partially, aided by the glint of metal. There was one very high window of course; General Takhnu was not so stupid as to construct an unventilated armory.

Grinning, Berneson edged over to the wall, paced out to the clear spot in the center of the floor, and nodded. He folded his arms, still grinning, and disappeared—

—to reappear in the bathroom of their suite. In the

act of talking, his two companions stared silently at him. Rinegar's eyes dropped to the dust on the other man's clothing.

"We're in business," Berneson said, brushing himself. "I've just popped in and out of the armory. They've got enough stuff down there to murder every person and worg on Bor!"

Cory shuddered, glancing at Rinegar, who turned thoughtfully away. "Umm. All right. Then what?"

"Then this: Did you get when the prisoners are being loaded into the ship?"

Rinegar turned back, looking old. "I—I don't want to tell you."

Berneson nodded. "Right, then. And tomorrow we get taken back to our hotel—except that we won't, because you'll be incriminated, because of what *I* am going to do *tonight*. Except that you won't be incriminated either," he went on, his tone harsh and nasty and his eyes fixed on the older man, "because you'll be blown up with the rest of them."

"Bernie!" Cory started forward.

He shrugged. "If we can't save the conscripts—and I certainly won't break my back teeporting them all outside somewhere, one at a time—we can't. I'll just blow up the armory. Up goes Takhnu, up goes the whole complex, including Borean prisoners and—you."

"The loading was scheduled for tonight," Rinegar said quietly. "As soon as the boys were brought in and . . . 'processed.' They're probably all aboard the ship by now."

Berneson thought about that, then slapped his hands together, grinning broadly. "That's *wonderful!* Jake: go to bed. At least get into nightclothes. Leave the water running in the bathroom and close the doors on both sides. Cory, there's no hall door from your room; I looked. Go in and put on nighclothes. If someone shows up, checking on us, Jake, you tell them Cory's in bed and I'm in the bathroom. Surely they won't break into the bathroom to verify that! See you later."

"Bernie—"

But the smiling man was gone again, and Cory and Rinegar exchanged unequivocally anxious looks before Cory went swiftly into the bathroom, locked the door, and entered her own room. She sat there listening to the noisy bathroom.

Berneson, meanwhile, rematerialized in the armory. A brief search got him what he wanted, and he strapped a holstered hand-whistler on his hip. Then he took a deep breath, closed his eyes, concentrated strongly, and vanished—

—and was in the Azuli spaceship's emergency airlock. He had been certain of its location, and it seemed the one place he could be certain of appearing without being seen. He sighed out his breath, took another, and let it go. Drawing the sonic pistol, he opened the lock's inner door.

"Miserable security," he muttered, emerging into an unlighted passageway. "But I'd hardly expected to find anyone in the emergency hatch—which should be just below the hold!" He stood very still, listening.

Clearly to his ears came the sound of voices, all speaking unaccented Borean. They came from overhead. Grinning, he measured the height with his eyes, made a judgment as to the thickness of the plate forming the hold "floor" and his "ceiling," and . . . teleported.

He materialized atop a Borean boy so horror-stricken he could not even cry out. Others did, backing away as Berneson and his unwilling cushion sprawled. Berneson sorted them out. Then he gripped

the shivering boy's shoulder and put his face close to
the reddish-brown one.

"I," he said, "am Baffling Berneson, the Man with
the X-Ray Eyes. And I'm sorry I hurt you—I came to
help, not hurt."

"Berneson!"

He turned. "Hi, Junty. *Sh*, now, no yelling."

Berneson rose, looked around, and cleared his
throat to begin his speech. He had thought it would be
a hard job convincing these passive, complacent people that they must do what he wanted. He was pleas-
antly surprised. Many of the young of Bor were no
longer so complacent or passive. Hunted, stolen,
taken *somewhere,* they had reacted as humans, whether
Earthside or Borean: some in terror, others in action or
readiness for it.

Once they'd got the gist of his plan, seventeen of
them started crowding forward. They represented the
Sons of Freedom—and two other organizations of
draft resisters. They'd be enough, he knew, even if the
others wouldn't go along.

"All right, cousins. Get back against the bulkhe—
the walls, *Stay* back. I'm going to start popping in and
out of here, and there's going to be a stack of weapons right here in very short order!"

16

"I hope," Berneson said, "that my taking only weapons from the rear of the armory will keep the loss
from being discovered, if anyone checks."

"How d'you know it was the rear?" Rinegar asked.

Berneson shrugged, smiling. "No doors. The prisoners' hold on that ship now contains enough weaponry to take on every Azuli here—if those Borean idiots could be counted on to shoot and shoot straight. I'm worried they'll zap each other, so I provided arms to only twenty of them. Ready to go?"

"Ah—Bernie," Cory said, wearing a minuscule smile, "you have, ah, neglected to fill us in on the Berneson Plan."

He looked at her as though she'd said something preposterously stupid. "We're going to the ship. We're taking it over. We're getting off Bor—and the armory's going up, which will get the Azuli off Bor, too!" He shook his head. "What'd you think, I was planning a performance for the prisoners?"

"And—and just how do you propose to get me on that ship, Bernie?" Rinegar asked. Regretfully, he patted his paunch.

"Been thinking about that, Jake. Too bad you didn't *stop* eating, rather than cutting down. You must've gained another five pounds slopping up that Azuli dinner tonight! Well. Cory: if I teeport you to a specific place, then come back here, can you add your Power to mine?"

"Oh *Bernie*—yes. Yes, I think so!"

"*Think* so," Rinegar snapped. "Now wait a—"

But Bernie was already scooping the girl up in his arms. "See you," he told the other man, and vanished.

"Don't make a sound," Berneson whispered to the girl. "We're in the armory—because it's a good intermediate point. I didn't dare teeport all the way out—be bad to wind up *in* the wall! Look around. Where we were is—that way."

She nodded.

"Ready to go?"

"Ready to go, Bernie," she said, clinging to his neck, and she had that strange rushing disoriented redout sensation again—and they were back in the suite, facing Rinegar. She smiled.

"This is going to take coordination," Berneson said, putting her down. "When I say *go,* you make the mental effort to lift ole Jake here, and to transport him to the armory. Meanwhile I'll try to lift him physically and teeport. We work as a team, right?"

She nodded.

"I . . . wish you would stop saying 'try,' " Rinegar said anxiously.

Berneson pointed. "Stand on that chair, please. I'm not going to try to carry you as I did her, potato-sack! I'll grab you around the thighs and you just go limp over my shoulder, all right? And if we come down hard, bite your tongue, because we'll be in the armory."

"The *armory!*"

"Cory?"

"Ready, Bernie. Oh, Bernie—"

"Ready . . . get set . . . *go!*"

Berneson wrapped both arms around the bigger man's thighs, pulling, then grunting as the weight came down on his shoulders. At the same time he thought himself—with great urgency!—back into the clear space in the center of the armory floor. And he was there, and his legs gave away, and he and Jake were on the floor, grunting.

"You all right, Jake?"

"I . . . bit my lip instead of my tongue," Rinegar announced. "It's bleeding. Bernie—"

"Stand over there. Do *not* move, and do *not* make a sound, *please!* Be right back."

"Bernie—"

But Bernie had already vanished. Rinegar hauled himself to his feet with a suppressed grunt. Limping a little, he moved over beside the double stack of crates Berneson had indicated.

Berneson reappeared in the suite's bathroom in time to see the hall door open. Colonel Skarsh and two others, both with side arms and one carrying a heavy-duty whistler, entered. Trouble!

"I'm sorry to tell you," Skarsh said, "that all sree of you are under arrest—*where's Rinegar?*"

"Arrest? Rinegar? What the—why, Cousin Colonel? What's your interest in us?"

Skarsh gave him a tight smile, holding his pistol steady on Berneson's midsection. "I want to discuss your talents, of course," he said. "Oh—and I want to see how pale you are, under your clothing."

Bernie sighed. "Right," he said. "It's all over, huh?"

"It is all over, *cousin,*" Skarsh said, his smile broadening. "You *are* Eartsiders, sen!" He stood there smiling in triumphant delight a moment, then said, "And perhaps you'd be kind enough to tell me where you came by sat Azuli gun—*and do not reach for it.*"

Berneson nodded equably. "Oh yes, the gun. Well, I teepörted into the armory, you see."

"You—you're a—"

At that moment one of Skarsh's men cried out, pointing. Skarsh jerked his head to follow the man's outstretched finger—in time to see the smallest of the room's chairs leap up from the floor, waver in air a moment, and rush toward them. In unthinking reaction, Skarsh raised his gun and triggered at the chair. Then he ducked, twisting toward Berneson.

"*Kill him!*" Skarsh shouted. "*He's an eartsider teeporter!*"

Berneson wasn't there. As soon as Corisande mind-lifted the chair and threw it at the Azuli, Berneson teeported across the room. He had his pistol half out when he landed, just beside the door. He kicked it shut. The Azuli spun. Berneson ordered them to drop their guns, saw there was no hope of that, saw his death in their eyes and their weapons, and he used his gun, three times.

As though in shock, he stood there gazing down at three Azuli bodies. "Well," he muttered. "That pretty much puts a cap on things, doesn't it?" He turned and locked the door. "C'mere, Cory, let's get out of here."

With the trembling girl in his arms, Berneson tele-ported back into the armory.

"What kept you?" Rinegar muttered. They told him. Then Cory bent forward, squinting in the darkness, to peer at the stack of cases beside him.

"Bernie! Grenades! If you could take several of them back—"

"Back there? And then what? Activate them and hope I can teeport out fast enough?"

She shook her head. "No—just take them there and return. *I* will activate them from here, by poltie-Power."

"Can you do that?"

"I think so. Little lost if I can't—Wait! All we have to do is go outside and throw them! I'll mind-direct them through the windows."

He shook his head. "No you won't. No mind-sent grenade's going to break those windows. I wouldn't even bet that concussion from one of them would." He looked around, then made a face and reached for the crate. "All right. Back I go. After tonight, I'll sleep for a week!"

"Wait a moment," Rinegar said. "Take these." He

indicated the top packing case in the second stack. "They're grenades too—*gas* grenades."

Bernie grinned. "Yesss!" He tested the crate's weight. "Isn't that nice. No more than fifty pounds; I'll just take the whole case." Picking it up, he vanished—

—and reappeared within a minute. But already Cory and Jake had another case open, and Cory was studying a grenade. She nodded. "These are the very simplest kind," she said. "Just pull this ring. The little pin on it that separates the acid from the powder comes out, they rush together, the powder flares, and up goes the charge." She looked at Berneson. "Uh— first let's get Rinegar to wherever we go next."

"I wish I weren't such a dead weight," Rinegar muttered apologetically.

"You're the one made it all possible by picking their brains, remember? All right, Cory. We've got to hurry, now. As soon as someone goes in and finds Skarsh and his friends—" He shook his head.

With Cory in his arms, he teleported out to the little clump of scoor-bush he had located, outside the wall and less than a quarter-kilometer from the looming spaceship. She looked around, nodded, and he teleported them back. Again they applied both their Powers, coupled with his muscle. Berneson fell into the scoor, dumping Rinegar: more grunts.

"Sorry," Berneson muttered, and teeported back for Cory.

She held the grenade again. "Bernie!" she whispered, jerking her head toward the building's front doors. From outside came the sound of loud Azuli voices: hourly sensor check showed warmth within the armory: a breaker-in! More voices, more noise; the door's being unlocked. Cory gazed at the grenade she held, seeming to fondle it, testing the ring-pull arming device. She looked at the stack of crates beside her. Then she closed her eyes. Berneson was practically jumping up and down, now, gun in hand as he gazed toward the front of the big metal warehouse, and the opening door. Cory opened her eyes.

"There went our lovely suite," she said. "Now us!"

Bernie lifted her swiftly just as the sound of the explosion began. Again she knew that decidedly unpleasant sensation that was teleportation: dematerialization/rematerialization, rather than physically moving through space and walls. Berneson's left foot came down on Rinegar's leg. Rinegar groaned loudly and both Bernie and Corisande fell. The three of them thrashed about in the prickly scoor.

Rising to hands and knees, Cory looked back at the great metal of the Azuli stronghold. She narrowed her eyes as she looked in the direction of the armory.

Concentrating, she squeaked when Berneson grabbed her and, holding her tightly, teleported.

She didn't have to ask where they were; they were surrounded by anxious-looking young men. "Ship's hold," Berneson told her. "Hullo troops, meet Corisande the Incredible. Stay where you are please; we'll be right back."

Corisande sagged when he returned her to the ground outside.

"I—I'm glad I'm a poltie," she stammered. "I *hate* teeporting! Oh—give me a moment—"

She broke off, twisting around to look at that two-story metal wall. Inside, flames licked at the air, rising above the wall. A siren was shrieking, and they could hear the shouts of many Azuli.

"We don't have a moment," Berneson told her, reaching for Rinegar. Sighing, she nodded, and a min-

ute later Berneson was back, having deposited the
other man in the ship's hold. He reached for Cory.

"Ber-nie . . . suppose I just pull the pin on one of
those grenades in the armory? From here?"

He thought about it. "Lovely idea. But the concussion might be enough to topple the ship. Uh-uh. Save
it for later."

And he took her into the hold with one hundred
Boreans and a waiting Rinegar. The others watched
enviously while she and Junty Grenn embraced.

"My dear friends," Berneson said grinning. "We
have just blown up the main headquarters building
and filled its husk and most of the Azuli complex with
toxic gas—of Azuli manufacture." He raised a hand,
touching another to his temple. "Please—no applause;
Berneson the Unfathomable has an unfathomed
headache. Anyhow, dear hearts, *we will now take
over this flaining ship!*"

17

It was very obvious to everyone that Berneson was enjoying himself immensely. It was also highly likely
that only a Berneson, a devil-may-care and profoundly immature and insecure prankster, could have accomplished what the trio of Earthsiders—Corberrin—had thus far accomplished. Certainly it was true
that the Azuli had not known they were psi's, which
made matters considerably simpler. Even at that, the
brush with the obviously very bright Colonel Skarsh
had made it a near thing, pointing up the insanity of

three people's declaring war on nearly three hundred.

But the three hundred were smugly secure in their knowledge that they were well out of the war zone, on a backward and pre-technological planet where risk to life and limb were minimal, and sabotage *within* their steel-walled keep quite impossible. Their chief concern had been disease, which was why every Azuli present at the dinner and subsequent performance had worn nasal filters. Too, they were not being attacked in a normal fashion by a normal foe. They were attacked swiftly, secretly, and by three persons with three separate psionic Powers.

Before General Takhnu had known there was a war on—here—he had lost his Intelligence aide, and his harmless prisoners had been rendered dangerous, with teleported arms. By the time his men knew of the danger, they had no general, indeed no officers, all of whom had gone up with the main building. Corisande had quite forgotten the girls the Azuli used as cooks and servants, and Berneson had not seen fit to remind her. They were what generals called "expected losses" and "necessary casualties," and just now Berneson was a general. Any of the building's occupants not killed in the explosion or by the collapsing structure itself had certainly been overcome by the gas from an entire crate of grenades.

That same gas was now eddying bluely throughout the compound, and more than one Azule suddenly collapsed as he and his fellows dashed madly about, seeking the source of the trouble and seeking orders. Azuli fighting men were trained much the same as those of the Earth Union: they were not to move without orders. But now there was no one above the rank of lieutenant to give orders. Once they realized this, the hyper-nervous lieutenants would take some control of the insanity—provided they survived the writhing, swirling gas.

As to the spaceship, already loaded with their farm conscripts and scheduled for liftoff the afternoon of the following day, it was a ridiculously simple matter. On board were ten guards, six Azuli in sickbay in the ship's cybernetic Doctor along with one medic to read the gauges, and a tech, laboriously making his final rounds before pronouncing the vessel spaceworthy. There was no need for anyone else's presence aboard. The compound was secure, the ship was secure, and the prisoners were secure in the locked hold—until Berneson teleported into the passageway.

Showing the two card-playing Azuli guards there his gun, he ordered them to unlock the hold's hatch. They did so, and soon they were inside, disarmed and still wondering what had happened.

What had happened, in less than ten minutes, was that the Azuli had lost a spaceship to ninety-nine primitives and three psi-Powered Earthsiders. They suffered one casualty, because the overly anxious and militant boy would not obey Berneson. He rounded a passageway corner and was burned down. The Azuli guard who took his life survived him by less than twenty seconds.

Rinegar had gone straight to Infirmary to study the six stricken Azuli there and to check the Doctor's record-tapes.

"Cory," Berneson said, "can you activate that grenade in the armory from here?"

She shook her head. "It's outside my range. No. I can't *feel* it."

"Then we'll have to get really mean," he said, shrugging, and was gone. She and the Boreans looked around, the latter with wide eyes. Despite the fact that they'd seen it several times previously this night, they still had no notion of what he was doing or how.

They felt the big ship quiver once, twice, and then again, by which time they were all shivering more than the craft itself.

Berneson reappeared. "Never used a spacer's belly-gun before," he said. "Molecule displacer. Took me two tries to get the proper range, even with all the ro-botracking system these fellows have. We have, I mean."

"Bernie? What—"

He shrugged. "Third shot was a direct hit on the armory. There is no longer an Azuli base on Bor. There are no longer any Azuli, either."

The ship was big enough not to shudder at the sound waves from the Borean cheers, but its steel passageways and cabins rang and rang again with the sounds and their echoes.

Berneson had to bellow for their attention.

"I want all of you, *all* of you, to run all the way to Sleespoken!" he shouted. "Tell them the Azuli are the deadliest enemy Bor has ever even dreamed of. Tell them that every boy taken off Bor is a slave on a far world, raising food to feed the worst enemy Bor has ever known. Tell them that Corberrin is from EARTH, a world called EARTH, and that we have saved Bor! Then bring them back, so we can give you all a guided tour of this pile of rivets!"

"Bernie-e-e-ee—"

He ignored Corisande. "Oh, wait, wait. There's a mechanism on the airlo—I mean door out of this thing, fellows, and I can't find the controls," he shouted. The Boreans stared. "You can't carry metal out of the ship. Just leave the guns, and we'll keep them right here for you."

One of the more militant Sons of Liberty was frowning, his knuckles pale as he gripped his gun. "Berneson—"

Berneson beamed at him, pointing. "Good man, Leert! You're the very one to lead! Here, show them the way." And Berneson reached for the boy's gun. Unable to stop himself, Leert passed it over.

Leaving their guns behind—Berneson personally checked each one—the ninety-nine Boreans hurried out of the airlock and down the ramp, shielding their eyes from the glare of the conflagration that had been Azul's slave base on their planet. When the last of them had begun to run as the shouting Leert directed, trotting backward and waving them on, Berneson glanced at Corisande with a boyish Berneson grin. He slapped the airlock control, waited for it to *chunk* shut, entered the ship, and closed the inner hatch. He watched its autolock spin.

"Bernie—you lied to them!"

He nodded.

"You're . . . not a very nice man, Bernie. Even as a hero."

"I've never pretended to be either, Cory. Had a lot of fun, though. Cory, Cory, we couldn't let those sillies go out on Bor with *guns!* Think about it. Some of those kids—pardon me, those young men—are really mad, and they're quite a gang. Think of that, too. And the likes of that wild-eyed Leert with—d'you think he'd have handed over his gun to me without a lie and a little salesmanship?"

"And—the guided tour?"

He shook his head. "They'll have to miss that. They won't make it back by our liftoff time, now will they?" He stepped forward to clamp a hand on each of her upper arms. "Where are you going, Cory?"

Rinegar, hurrying along the passageway, answered for her: "We're going *back!*" He was smiling—and so were his *eyes*. "You know what those six Azuli are suffering from?"

"Back where?"

"What?"

"I'll answer your question first, Cory. Their symptoms have been chest pains, a steadily worsening cough, and fever. PPLO, and I'd bet on it. But they don't know!"

"What's PPLO?" Cory asked.

"Cory, think a moment. Right after we arrived here we all three had some minor illness. Non-productive coughs, chest pain, low-grade fever, not enough to bother about. Gone immediately, and all we had were sore throats that lingered for a few days."

She nodded. "Of course I remember. We were scared about alien microbes and the possibility of our catching—Jake?" She cocked her head. "Are you saying that little whatsis we had is what's wrong with the Azuli? And it's *killing* them?"

He nodded. "A Borean bug totally alien to Azuli knowledge and understanding. PPLO: pleuro-pneu-monia-like organism. Maybe we've had previous exposure, on a subclinical basis. Or, maybe we've been inoculated and genetic-engineered against so many things that we may've been accidentally immunized against this one. My guess is the Azuli know all about bacteria, the 'normal' disease-causers, but maybe they haven't had any experience with viruses at all. The PPLO is a thingy about halfway between a virus and a bacterium. Apparently the Boreans are naturally immune; we are *almost* immune, and experienced only a bit of discomfort from it—and to the Azuli it's a *killer!*"

"Tough for them," Berneson said. He was staring

darkly at the other man. "Now my question. Going back to where?"

"Back to the war zone, Bernie! Back to—well, Quamar, I suppose, would be the best place. Think about it. I don't know what's with the Azuli—what do any of us know about them? They've always been 'the enemy.' PPLO is just alien to their medicine, I imagine. All right, we're all carrying that microorganism in us right now. Earthside medics can study us, isolate the thing, and—Look, there's probably an epidemic raging on their planet right now, carried in from here. And it's going to be *Earth* that offers to provide the cure, and the vaccine! We even have those two Azuli guards in the hold to work with, in developing the vaccine."

Corisande clapped her hands. "Oh Jake! The war will be over in *months! This* will show them who's not fit to help in the war," she added intensely. *"We'll* show them who's a reject and who isn't!"

But when she turned her elated gaze on Berneson, he was frowning.

18

Rinegar looked around as his two companions entered the control room. "We're in trouble."

"What—how?"

"The tower." He jerked his head.

"That thing over there that looks like an old-time gantry?" Berneson asked. "What about it? What's it for?"

"The Azuli are a cautious people," Rinegar told

him. That's an engine-release tower. This ship not only has to be cleared, it has to be released from that tower before it goes anywhere."

"Can't we override?"

"In about a month, maybe, if we worked day and night and found a way to 'deceive' the ship's computer. Here, I'll show you." And he did. When he pushed the button that bore only the two Azuli letters meaning START, a red light began flashing.

"You see? That's the—"

"Eartsider! So it *is* Eartsiders!"

They all jerked around; another light had come on, marked TOWER COM. The Azuli voice issued from the grille beneath it:

"How you have done what you have done I cannot understand. But—"

"You in the tower," Berneson snapped, bending to the grille. "Listen. We've blown up your entire base. Takhnu, all of them, they're *gone*. You're all alone. There isn't another Azuli left alive on Bor. Now *release this ship,* or we'll zap you and your tower with the ship's guns."

There was a long silence from the grille while the Azule in the tower, presumably the last of his race on this planet, pondered that. The three Earthsiders exchanged looks of nervous anxiety. They controlled the ship's antigrav, but the tower controlled thrust—and they needed thrust to get off this planet. The Azuli were indeed a cautious people!

And then the Azuli controller replied.

"Zap away, Eartsiders! And you will *never* leave sis planet!"

Rinegar found the control that cut off the pickup of the in-ship mike connected with the tower controller's pickup. He raised distressed eyes to the others. "We'll have to storm the tower." Then he returned his attention to the Azuli spaceship's controls, at last focusing the viewers. They were looking at the tower on the screen, and their gasps came almost in unison.

The tower whose operator decided whether the cautious Azuli—and now Corberrin—lifted off was quite nearby, quite tall, and armed. Certainly the Azule within had a view of the surrounding terrain. There would be no sneaking up on him, and there would be no storming that tower, not by three persons. They could destroy it, yes; the ship's guns would make short work of it. But they might never get their ship off the ground, much less into space.

The operator had a clear view of their ship, too, they saw. And he had armament. Even as Ringer tuned him in on the port viewscreen, a big gun was swiveling ponderously toward them. The last Azule on Bor had no hope of leaving, because he had no hope of wresting the ship away from the Earthside trio. Therefore he could only carry out the ugly rite of vengeance.

He could destroy them and the ship.

Berneson stared at the screen, looked briefly at Corisande, whose teeth were firmly set in her lower lip, and at Ringer: the big man seemed suddenly very old and stooped. Berneson thought: of the infection, of the war, of Earth and of his own planet, Mars. At last he heaved a great desolate sigh.

"Well. Now this isn't fun. But—I told you before that I didn't want to go back. So, activate the antigrav and stand by for liftoff!"

"Bernie—!"

But he had vanished—

—to reappear in the tower control chamber. Again his Borean luck had held—at least in getting him safely into the square, controls-filled room where he had never been. But, just as there had been in that first teleported trip into the armory, there was a hitch. There were two roller chairs in the room, and Berneson came down on—in—one of them. The chair rolled. Berneson sprawled. The Azuli pistol he held rapped the floor sharply when his forearm did. Pain shot jagged needles up through his arm and it was all he could do to hang onto the pistol.

The hitch should have been a minor one. The chair Berneson had landed in was behind the Azule in the other chair, squinting at a round screen that was most probably his fire-control scanner. At the crash and the grunt and smacking sound behind him, he spun half around in his swivel chair. He should have panicked, seeing the armed Earthsider there on the floor, materialized in the control room as by sorcery.

He did not. Without looking away from Berneson, the Azule shot out one hand to scoop up the little needle gun on the work area before him. He swung it, triggered it.

Berneson's eyes went very wide and he gasped. His mouth sagged open. Staring at the Azule, he triggered his own gun. The Azule had a needler, Berneson a microminiaturized whistler. The Azule died instantly.

Gasping, unable to close his mouth because breath was so terribly dear and so fleeting, Berneson dropped his gun and reached for the edge of the desk. Strength and extraordinary will power enabled him to drag himself up. One glance told him the big gun lining up on the ship was on full automatic, and he slapped it off, nearly falling with the minor exertion. He forced himself to pause, opening his mouth wide to drag in another hard-fought and painful breath.

Had the needle struck anywhere near him, it would

have released a small charge of poison gas that he might have avoided by holding his breath and getting swiftly away from it. But it had not been one needle, but two, and they had not struck near him. They had both hit him, penetrating tunic and flesh beneath. Now they were busily dissolving, sending not gas but liquid poison through his system.

Thrust into a cybernetic Doctor within something like one minute, Berneson would have had a forty percent chance of living.

He poised his palm over the green button. Thick as his thumb, it was the release for the ship's thrusters; the antigrav, of course, Ringar would already have activated. The spaceship was like an old balloon, straining at its moorings, awaiting that small amount of thrust it needed to leap up from Bor.

"All circuits—open," he said, making an effort to sound natural and coherent. His throat felt as though he had swallowed a great lump of dough filled with numbing analgesics. And someone seemed to be standing on his chest, crushing his lungs. "Strap . . . in!"

"Strapped in," Ringar's voice came back, "but Bernie! You can't lift us off. You'll be left behind."

"Told—you I . . . didn't want to . . . go back!"

"*Bernie!*" Corisande's voice this time, rising high and shrill in her sudden apprehension. "What's wrong?"

The breath he fought for and won, like a landed fish, seemed to take ten minutes to suck in. "Nothing's . . . wrong, stupid," he said, letting the breath out slowly with the words and leaning close to the speaker. "All—I have to do is . . . teeport back . . . over there the mo—ment I push this green . . . button. If I . . . don't, you'll know I de . . . cided . . . to ssstayyy. . . ."

His palm jammed down on the green button. The image of the ship on the screen was a wavering, shivering misty-red.

"Bernie!" Rinegar snapped, as he too realized the other man's voice was not normal.

"Bernieeeeee!" Corisande's cry was a shriek.

"Go win . . . the war . . . heroes," Berneson said. "You know . . . I . . . hate being a . . . he-e-e-ro-o-oh. . . ." He expelled the last of his breath with the final word. He saw the ship, misty and shuddery, begin to tremble. Then there was a gout of flame beneath it and it shivered again, suddenly sitting on a flattened golden capsule of fire like a hen setting a golden egg. The egg fattened, became a sphere, then an upended capsule. The ship was dancing, rising, seeming to lift very slowly—

"Ber-nie-e-e-ee. . . ."

Berneson did not answer because he could not. There was no way his closed throat could suck in one more breath to speak. Or to live.

The screaming voice faded and then was gone as the big spaceship rushed up from Bor and out into space to end a nineteen-year war.

Four Outstanding
Science Fiction Collections
from Laurel-Leaf Library

THREE TRIPS IN TIME AND SPACE □
Larry Niven, John Brunner, Jack Vance
Three award-winning authors respond to the
challenge of space/time travel. 95¢

THE SCIENCE FICTION BESTIARY □
Robert Silverberg, editor
Nine stories by science fiction masters,
from light and humorous to spine-tingling. 95¢

MIND TO MIND □
Robert Silverberg, editor
This collection of nine stories includes such masters
as Isaac Asimov, C. M. Kornbluth, Algis Budrys,
and Poul Anderson. 95¢

BEYOND CONTROL □
Robert Silverberg, editor
Seven thematically linked stories provocatively
treat the dangers of technology run rampant. 95¢

LAUREL-LEAF LIBRARY
The paperbacks young readers love most!

☐ **MAVERICKS Jack Schaefer**
Illustrations by Lorence Bjorklund
"In a magnificent tribute to a vanishing breed of men and
horses, the author of *Shane* takes us back to the old
Southwest. His mavericks are the invincible mustangs and
hard riding cowboys of New Mexico. A superb book."
—*Horn Book*   95¢

☐ **ARE YOU THERE GOD? IT'S ME, MARGARET.**
Judy Blume
Margaret Simon, going on twelve, has a lot to worry about.
Making friends in a new school, boys, dances, school
projects, growing up physically "normal"—and choosing
a religion.   95¢

☐ **CHIEF Frank Bonham**
The gripping struggle of a band of California Indians
to survive in the present.   95¢

☐ **FRIEDRICH Hans Peter Richter**
Trapped in Hitler's Nazi Germany, a young Jewish boy
struggles to survive.   95¢

☐ **HEY, DUMMY Kin Platt**
A moving story about a young boy's attempt to save a
retarded child.   95¢